PUFFIN BOOKS

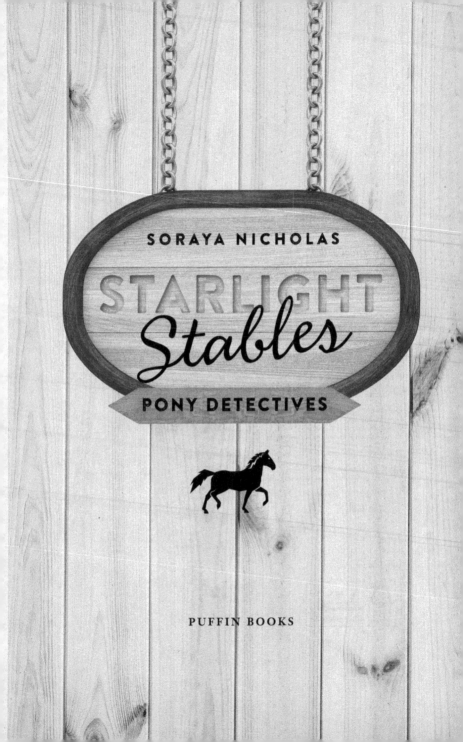

SORAYA NICHOLAS

STARLIGHT
Stables

PONY DETECTIVES

PUFFIN BOOKS

PUFFIN BOOKS

UK | USA | Canada | Ireland | Australia
India | New Zealand | South Africa | China

Penguin Books is part of the Penguin Random House group of companies
whose addresses can be found at global.penguinrandomhouse.com.

Penguin
Random House
Australia

First published by Penguin Random House Australia Pty Ltd, 2016.

Design by Marina Messiha © Penguin Random House Australia Pty Ltd
Cover photograph © Caitlin Maloney, Ragamuffin Pet Photography
Printed and bound in Australia by Griffin Press, an accredited ISO AS/NZS 14001
Environmental Management System's printer.

National Library of Australia Cataloguing-in-Publication data:

Nicholas, Soraya, author.
Starlight stables : pony detectives / Soraya Nicholas.

978 0 1433 0861 4 (paperback)

For children.
Ponies--Juvenile fiction.
Friendship--Juvenile fiction.

A823.4

puffin.com.au

For my gorgeous boys, Mackenzie and Hunter.
As a girl, I always dreamed of living on a farm,
surrounded by dogs and horses, and I hope you
never take for granted how lucky you are to have
those things growing up.

CHAPTER ONE

Starlight Stables

Poppy sucked in a breath and looked around the farm. She watched the mares in the paddock with their foals at foot, kicking up their hooves as they played in the midday sun. Tears sprang into her eyes but she bit down hard on her lip, clutching her bag tighter to her chest.

'Poppy?'

She smiled and turned, searching for her aunt.

'Pop! I'm so happy you're here!' Aunt Sophie ran across the yard from the stables, arms open, her crazy-happy dog Casper bouncing at her side. Her long blonde hair was braided in a plait and slung over her shoulder, and she was dressed in her

1

usual cream jodhpurs and a shirt.

Poppy dropped her bag so her aunt could hug her, trying hard not to cry. She let her cheek be kissed, and held on tight. Coming here was supposed to be fun, the best holiday ever, but she couldn't stop thinking about home.

'Let me look at you.' Aunt Sophie stood back, hands on her hips.

Poppy couldn't help it. She did burst into tears then. They rolled like big raindrops down her cheeks, and she dropped to her knees to give Casper a cuddle. The Australian shepherd was soft and snuggly, and she could have held on to him all day, even if he was trying to lick her face.

'Oh, sweetheart, it's okay. Come here.' Aunt Sophie pulled her back up, and Poppy tucked into her side as she hugged her again.

'You missing your dad?' Aunt Sophie asked.

Poppy nodded, even though that wasn't quite right. She didn't want to talk about it, not to anyone. She wasn't lying, she did still miss her dad, all the time, but it was her mum she was worried about. She knew she shouldn't have left her, but she hadn't been to Starlight Stables for so long, and she missed all the horses so bad.

'I'm sorry we had to get one of the helpers to pick you up from the train station,' Aunt Sophie said.

Poppy was grateful for the change of subject and smiled at her aunt, blinking away the last of her tears. Aunt Sophie picked up Poppy's bag and steered her toward the stables.

'But we had a good reason, Pop. Come on, we've got something to show you.'

Something to show her? 'Do you have a new riding school horse?' Poppy asked.

Aunt Sophie grinned and gave Poppy's shoulders a squeeze. 'Something better.'

What could be better than a new horse? Poppy walked faster alongside her aunt, eager to reach the stables. She hadn't seen the horses in ages, and she couldn't wait to be around them again, to forget everything and just enjoy her four-legged friends.

'Hey, Popster!'

'Hi, Uncle Mark.' Poppy couldn't help feeling shy when he ran out of the stables and gave her a smacking kiss on the top of her head. Bending low, he scooped her up in a big bear hug so that her feet left the ground. She always loved the horsey smell of him and the way she disappeared into his arms as he held her tight.

'Has Sophie let you in on the secret?' he asked as he lowered her to the floor, dark brown eyes locked on hers.

Poppy shook her head. 'No.'

She watched as her aunt and uncle looked at one another. Something was definitely up. Poppy followed them into the stables as they walked down the aisle between the stalls, but she couldn't keep up with them. She had to stop and reach out a hand to each nose, stroke the soft skin of each horse's muzzle as she passed them. She knew every single one of them, and she loved them all equally.

'Hey, Jupiter.' Poppy paused slightly longer at his stall – maybe she loved Jupiter a teensy bit more than the others, she admitted to herself. She pressed a kiss to his massive chestnut cheek as he hung over the stable door, munching his hay. His muzzle smelt sweet – a combination of his hard feed and just that great horse smell that she loved so much. She'd missed it.

'Pop?' Aunt Sophie prompted from outside another stable.

She'd almost forgotten about the surprise while she was giving Jupiter a scratch. 'I'm coming,' she said as she pulled away from Jupiter and ran past the rest of the stalls, sending out silent apologies to the other horses, and promising that she'd come see them soon.

She reached her aunt and uncle and skidded on some hay because she stopped so fast. 'Who's this?' she asked. A pretty grey face was peeking over the last stall, its big brown eyes watching her, like she was trying to figure out what was going on, too. The ponies weren't usually down here – this part of the stable block was for the bigger horses.

Aunt Sophie laughed and gave Poppy a nudge forward. 'This is Crystal.'

'She's beautiful.' Poppy stroked her face and giggled as Crystal blew on her cheek and nuzzled her hair.

'I think she likes you,' Uncle Mark said, leaning over to pat the pony. Poppy loved how gentle he was with animals. He was the local big-animal vet, and she liked nothing more than going out with him on call-outs when she was staying at the farm, seeing him in action.

Poppy looked over her shoulder. 'Is she boarding here?' she asked.

Aunt Sophie shook her head. 'Crystal just arrived, Poppy. She's your surprise.'

Poppy's stomach flip-flopped. What did her aunt mean, her surprise?

Uncle Mark took a step closer and slung an arm around Poppy's shoulder. 'You've had a hard time this year, Poppy, and we wanted to do something for you.'

Poppy didn't want to think about the last year. All she *did* want was to think about horses and only horses. 'So I can ride her while I'm here?'

'Well, she's your pony, so I guess that means you can ride her whenever you like.'

Poppy spun around and looked from her uncle to her aunt. 'What?'

They were both laughing.

'The polite thing to say would be "thank you".' Aunt Sophie was smiling but her face was serious.

'My new pony?' Poppy asked, just in case she'd misheard. This was crazy! She'd been dreaming of her own pony for years.

'Get in there and meet her properly, kiddo,' said

Mark. 'Unless you don't like her?'

Poppy didn't need telling twice. She swiped the latch to Crystal's stall and stepped inside. 'Crystal.' She breathed out her name as if it were magical.

It couldn't be real. She couldn't be hers, could she? Her own pony? Poppy looked from her uncle to her aunt and back to Crystal again. Crystal, quite possibly the most beautiful, gorgeous, cutest pony Poppy had ever seen.

Crystal stepped closer to Poppy and blew on her hand, the pony's whiskers tickling Poppy's skin. Poppy threw herself at her aunt and uncle, squealing.

'Thank you, thank you, thank you!'

Whinnies and snorts echoed around the stables.

'Whoa, girl, you're scaring the horses!' Uncle Mark warned, but with a grin on his face.

'So, let's have a look at this pony, shall we?' Aunt Sophie said as she pulled a new pink lead rope from the door and handed it to Poppy.

Poppy took the pink rope and gently pulled it over Crystal's head. She was smiling from ear to ear. She just couldn't believe it. She'd been dreaming of owning her own horse since she could say the word, saving every cent to put toward her horse fund. But when her dad had died and they'd had to move, she'd given up. There was no way her mum was ever going to be able to afford a horse, or even help care for one.

But now Uncle Mark and Aunt Sophie had given her her very own pony.

If she hadn't been feeling so worried about her mum back home, it would have been the best day of her life.

Poppy led Crystal out to the arena. The pony walked obediently beside her, even though Poppy was feeling jumpy. It felt like ages since she'd last ridden, and she hoped she hadn't forgotten anything.

'Let's just take it easy today, okay?' said her aunt, opening the gate for them to pass through.

Poppy nodded. She would do whatever she was told, so long as it didn't mean leaving Crystal's side.

Crystal stood patiently, her head turned in to Poppy.

'Hey, miss,' Poppy murmured, stroking Crystal softly on the neck. 'Be kind to me today, huh? I haven't ridden in a while.'

She used to come here all the time, every school

holiday and long weekend, but it had been months since her last ride.

'You ready?' Aunt Sophie stood behind her, her face turned from nice aunt to serious instructor.

'Yup.'

Poppy pushed her left foot firmly into the stirrup and swung up, landing smoothly in the saddle. She was pleased Crystal had stayed still. Nothing beat good manners when it came to ponies. Next, she gathered up the reins and squeezed her lower legs against Crystal's side, asking her to walk on.

'We don't need to push it, but I want to check that you work well as a team. Technically, we've got her on trial for two weeks, so if she's not right, we can always take her back.'

Poppy almost swallowed her tongue. Take her back? There was no way she was going to give back her horse! She loved her too much already.

'Has she jumped before?' Poppy asked. Poppy loved jumping. Her dream had always been to make the Australian Young Rider Eventing squad by the time she was seventeen. She could just imagine them travelling around the country, competing at all the top competitions.

'Are you kidding? Crystal is famous around here.'

Poppy pulled back lightly on the reins, sitting deeper in the saddle at the same time, and Crystal came to a halt. 'What do you mean?' she asked.

'Poppy, we've had our eye on Crystal for a year now,' Sophie explained. 'The only reason we managed to get her for you is because her rider is leaving for university. She's been too tall for Crystal for a while, but she didn't want to sell her until now.'

Poppy felt her brow knit together as she thought about what her aunt had said. She could understand why someone wouldn't want to sell Crystal – she was a special pony, Poppy could tell that already. She'd be heartbroken if she ever had to sell a horse she loved. She asked Crystal to walk on and wondered, had they really been planning on getting her a pony all this time? She was so excited, her hands were all shaky.

'How come I've never seen her before?' Poppy asked. She didn't recognise Crystal, and she never forgot a horse she liked.

'Her owner would have been past low-level games and eventing when you started riding here,' Aunt Sophie said.

Poppy asked her to. Poppy squeezed her legs against Crystal's side to make her trot. Crystal responded, moving perfectly around the all-weather arena. It was like Crystal was reading her mind!

'Great, you two look fantastic!' Sophie said.

Poppy knew she had a stupid grin planted on her face and lost focus for a second, but Crystal never put a hoof wrong.

'Canter on now, Poppy,' Sophie instructed.

Poppy sat deep in the saddle, her heels planted down and her outside leg sliding back to ask for a canter. It happened like magic. Crystal gracefully balanced into a rolling canter with her inside leg leading, just like it was supposed to. They really were a team.

'Okay, bring her back to a walk and then in to the middle.'

Poppy did as she was told. Once they had stopped she took her feet out of the stirrups and bent forward, wrapping her arms around Crystal's neck.

'So, what do you think?' Sophie asked.

'I love her, Aunt Sophie,' Poppy gushed. 'She's the best pony in the world.'

'Do you think I'll be able to event her?'

'The past two years running, Crystal has taken out the eventing and show jumping local champs. She's a one-in-a-million pony, and we think you'll be out competing soon. If that's still what you want?'

Was Sophie truly talking about *her* new pony? Crystal was already a champion?

Poppy bit her lip. She was doing that a lot lately. Of course she still wanted to compete, but she couldn't leave her mum for long. If she did, who would look after her little brother? Tom had gone away with his best friend's family for the two weeks Poppy was at Starlight, so she knew he was okay for now. But if she stayed longer...?

'Okay, enough chitter chatter. Let's see how she goes for you,' Aunt Sophie called out. 'Now, I know you haven't been in the saddle for a while, so just push her slowly through her paces.'

Poppy tried to blank out everything from her mind and focus on Crystal. The pony had one ear flicked back, listening out for her, and Poppy whispered to her, comforting her.

'We can do this. Just take it nice and steady.'

Crystal snorted but moved forward as soon as

CHAPTER TWO

Crystal

'How are things going at home, Poppy?' Aunt Sophie asked over dinner.

Poppy pushed some spaghetti around her plate with her fork. She didn't want to talk about home, not even with Aunt Sophie. Her and Uncle Mark were pretty cool, for adults, but it didn't mean she wanted to tell them what it was really like.

'Um, good. You know.' Her words came out as a mumble.

'Good, or just okay?' Uncle Mark asked.

Poppy stuffed the spaghetti in her mouth to avoid having to answer. She wasn't ready to tell anyone about what it was like at home. This holiday was the only thing she wanted to talk about, otherwise she'd get all sad and need to phone her mum again.

'Your brother's off on holiday with a friend from school?' Aunt Sophie prompted.

Poppy nodded and swallowed the spaghetti. 'Uh-huh. He's at a friend's holiday home for a bit.'

'So how about Crystal, huh? You really like her?'

Poppy looked up and Uncle Mark winked at her from across the table, like he was trying to say it was okay to avoid the subject of home. Her shoulders went from being all tight and bunched to relaxed. She didn't mind talking about Crystal at all.

'She's amazing. Cantering on her was like being on a giant rocking horse.' That made them all laugh, and suddenly Poppy felt comfortable again.

'Well, you deserve her, Pop. I know how long you've been dreaming of a horse of your own.'

Poppy beamed. 'So can I ride her every day, or do you need me to do riding school stuff?' Poppy wanted to know exactly how much time she was going to be able to spend with her pony. She loved all the horses, but Crystal already felt more special somehow.

'We know you've had a whole lot of excitement today already, but Mark and I have something else we want to talk to you about,' Aunt Sophie said.

Hmmm. This didn't sound good. When adults wanted to 'talk', it usually ended in something bad. Poppy had firsthand experience of that. She looked down again at her spaghetti and waited for whatever was coming.

'We have two weeks booked for the riding camp as usual, and we're counting on your help again.'

Poppy nodded, tucking a loose strand of long hair behind one ear. She loved helping out with the riding school camp. Now that she was twelve, she was allowed to instruct the little ones and be second in charge to Sophie on trail rides. At least, that's what her aunt had said on the phone.

'But...'

Here it comes, Poppy thought.

'We've been wanting to do something special for some young riders the last couple of years, and buying Crystal for you sort of spurred us on. We know what it's like to want your own horse more than anything else in the world, and we're also looking to expand the riding school.'

Poppy looked from Uncle Mark to Aunt Sophie. She had no idea what they were talking about or where this conversation was going, which was making her nervous.

'We've purchased two other ponies. Well, taken them on trial first, actually, just like Crystal.'

'You're not going to send her back, are you?' Poppy felt like she might be sick. Not having a horse was bad enough, but getting one and then having her taken away would be her worst nightmare.

'No! Of course not,' Sophie said. 'It's completely up to you to decide if Crystal is the right pony for you. No one can take her away if you want her, but, if you don't like her, we'll find another.'

Phew! 'I've already decided that she's perfect.' Poppy had said it before, but she wanted to make herself one hundred per cent clear, to be on the safe side.

Uncle Mark grinned and took over from Sophie. 'We have two young riders who we've chosen to receive a scholarship. We want to give them the same opportunity we've given you, to further their riding and have their own pony. Of course, you will be the only one actually to own a pony, but they will have to care for and ride theirs as if they are their own. Neither of their mounts will be ridden by anyone else at the riding school, and if it works out, then we hope you'll all be spending a lot more time here. Maybe even this entire school holiday.'

Poppy bit her lip. She'd do anything to spend more time at the farm, but that meant leaving her mum for longer, and she wasn't sure if she could. How would Tom cope without her? And a little part of her was… jealous. She told herself not to be silly. She was going to have friends to ride with, and it was great that her aunt and uncle were giving other kids the chance to have a horse they could call their own. Poppy had Crystal – it wasn't like they were threatening to let someone else ride her. But she couldn't help it. She *did* feel jealous. She'd wanted a horse for so long, and now two other riders were just going to get one, too?

'The two girls we've chosen are heading up here tomorrow, and we have our fingers crossed that you'll like them. We want the three of you to have fun together, and to eventually represent Starlight Stables as a team.'

Uncle Mark kept talking as he took his empty plate into the kitchen. Poppy followed her uncle.

She had to admit, their plans for her this holiday did sound like a whole heap of fun, even if she was worried about staying for so long. Aunt Sophie had always said that she would be ready for some real competitions once she turned twelve, and it was all starting to come true.

Uncle Mark smiled at Poppy. 'Happy?' he asked.

Poppy threw her arms around her uncle and squeezed him so tight he had to fight to get away.

'You're the best uncle in the world,' she whispered. And she meant it. Sometimes, she dreamed that Sophie and Mark were her parents, that she had a mum *and* a dad again, and lived with them all the time. But then it only made her feel guilty, because she loved her mum.

She just wished her mum would go back to how she used to be. Because Poppy didn't know how much longer she was going to be able to pretend like everything was okay.

'Can I give my mum a call?' Poppy asked Sophie as she walked out of the kitchen. She just wanted to make sure her mum wasn't missing her too much.

'Of course,' Aunt Sophie said. 'You call her whenever you like, you don't have to ask.'

'I'll just need to talk to her, about staying longer. Make sure she's...' Poppy paused, not wanting to say too much. 'I just want to talk to her.'

Aunt Sophie touched her arm, her smile as warm as her soft blue eyes. 'I already spoke to your mum, before we chose Crystal. I wouldn't have done this if she wasn't okay with it, and I've asked her if it's okay for you to stay longer.'

Poppy leaned into her aunt when she hugged her. 'So she knew about this?'

'Yes. She was thrilled for you, especially after everything you've all been through.' Aunt Sophie let her go, patting her arm as she walked away.

'I'll still just give her a quick call,' Poppy said, reaching for the phone. She was happy her mum knew, but she still wanted to hear her voice, make sure she was coping. And then she'd be able to figure out if Tom would be all right at home without her, so she could enjoy her stay at the farm, with Crystal, for a little while longer.

Poppy pushed the soft brush firmly along Crystal's shoulder, making her already gleaming coat even shinier in the morning sun. She still couldn't believe it. There was just something different about grooming her own pony, something so much more special. Running her hand down Crystal's legs, she brushed under her tummy, exploring every groove and indent.

Crystal turned her head and breathed on Poppy's arm, making her giggle. Poppy threw her arms around Crystal's neck again. She just couldn't stop touching her.

'You ready for a trail ride this morning?' she asked, and imagined Crystal saying 'yes' as she put the brush down.

She shielded her eyes against the low sun and looked over to the arena where Aunt Sophie was riding her big warm blood horse, Jupiter. Sophie had been riding for almost half an hour now, so she must be almost done, Poppy reckoned. She was training for the national dressage champs, and once they were finished, Sophie was going to take Jupiter on a short hack to stretch out his muscles. Poppy was hoping to tag along for the ride with Crystal. She'd purposely tied up outside the stable block today, on the concrete wash-down bay, so she could keep an eye on the arena.

Jupiter trotted smoothly over the sand, head tucked down on the bit, white foam frothing at the corners of his mouth. Poppy loved watching her aunt ride. Aunt Sophie was so graceful, so still, her body moving as one with her horse. It was like her aunt was glued to the saddle. Poppy desperately wanted to be that good.

Sophie made Jupiter round the arena's far corner and come to a halt – a dead stop from such a forward-moving trot. Then she made him walk on, before loosening the reins.

'Do you want to get Crystal saddled up and ready?' Sophie called out. The light breeze carried her voice, and she sounded closer than she was.

'Are you finished?' Poppy called back.

Aunt Sophie gave Jupiter a pat on the neck and swung her ankles from the stirrups to stretch her legs, walking closer. 'He's a little stiff today so I'm going to finish up now. Go saddle that pony and meet me out front.'

Poppy sprinted inside the stables to get her saddle, leaving Crystal tied up. She was going on her first proper trail ride with Crystal and she couldn't wait!

'Walk, Poppy!' called her aunt. 'No running near the stables, remember?'

Poppy threw one arm in the air and gave a thumbs up, slowing to a half-walk run. A low nicker caught her attention and her grin doubled in size. Crystal was already calling out to her, like she knew she was her new mum!

Crystal had her ears pricked, listening to Poppy and occasionally breaking into an excited jog.

'You guys are getting on well together,' observed Aunt Sophie.

Poppy sat a little straighter and patted Crystal on the shoulder. 'She feels great.'

'Do you want to trot?'

Oh yes. There was nothing better than trotting next to Jupiter. He was a whopping 17 hands high, which meant that his trot equated to cantering in the pony world, and she couldn't wait to go fast on Crystal.

'Yep, let's go!'

Aunt Sophie broke into an elegant working trot, and Poppy tried to do the same, before Crystal took it upon herself to canter to keep up with Jupiter. They bounced along under Sophie's watchful eye, trotting over the pine needles and around the odd fallen branch, a canopy of blue gums and pine trees surrounding them.

'There's a log coming up so go around. Don't feel you have to jump so soon if you don't want to,' Sophie said.

Poppy was listening but she had no intention of missing her first real jump on her pony. Crystal could see it coming, Poppy knew, but she held her in check, keeping their canter slow and steady. She waited for Sophie to pop over the log – Jupiter hardly lifted his legs from a trot – but Poppy had a feeling that Crystal intended to jump big.

Sophie had pulled up and was watching her, calling out to her to stay steady in the saddle. Poppy could hardly hear her, though. Excitement was building fast inside her, making her feel jittery.

Two strides out, one and jump! Poppy squeezed lightly with her legs and leaned forward as Crystal lifted up over the almost-white blue gum bough. She pushed her hands forward so that her pony could jump freely without Poppy pulling on her mouth.

Thump. They landed perfectly on the other side. Poppy pulled back to a walk as she heard Sophie clapping.

'Well done! You were both perfect,' Sophie said.

Poppy beamed. This was the sort of pony she could do anything on. They would win ribbons, take out local championships and be the envy of all others. She intended to do everything she could to make Crystal love her, too, so the pony would try her best for Poppy in return.

'Keep that up and we might enter you in the show jumping at the gymkhana,' Sophie said.

The gymkhana? Poppy knew that the big Pony Club Gymkhana was on the last weekend before school started, and she calculated in her head how long that gave her to perfect her jumping. It would mean she'd be at the farm for four weeks. She gulped. As much as she wanted to stay and ride, she still wasn't sure about being away from home for so long, for the entire holidays.

'Would I be here the whole time until then?' Poppy asked her aunt.

'I was thinking you could go home for a few days, after the two weeks we'd already planned.

But then you'd come back for the rest of the break. Does that sound okay to you?' Aunt Sophie asked.

Poppy nodded. 'I think so.' She wasn't going to tell her aunt her worries, not yet.

'Can I definitely compete?' asked Poppy as they walked off down the homebound trail. She had only ever competed in her aunt's riding school games-day before now. Poppy knew Sophie would only let her compete in the local Pony Club Gymkhana if she thought she was truly ready for it, and that sent shivers of excitement down Poppy's spine.

'Of course. It'll be the first competition for you three girls as a team.'

Poppy felt a bit nervous about meeting the other girls. She thought about her best friend Sarah back home. Sarah didn't even like the look of horses, but she was heaps of fun to hang out with. Poppy had tried so hard to get her to come here to the summer camp, but Sarah had just rolled her eyes and said no every single time. Luckily, they both had their own phones now, which meant they could text each other at least. The phones were only supposed to be for emergencies – their mums had given them each a phone for Christmas, now that they walked to school on their own – but Poppy and Sarah managed to get away with texting each other while Poppy was away. She couldn't wait to message her and fill her in on these new girls.

Poppy realised that Sophie was still talking to her. 'There'll be four local pony clubs competing this year,' Sophie said.

'Are you still running the Starlight gymkhana this summer before the big Pony Club one?' Poppy asked as they rode side by side down the wider part of the trail, the sun shining down on her arms now the trees became more sparse closer to the farm.

Sophie nodded and turned in her saddle to look at her.

'Of course! All of my pupils are looking forward to it, and it'll be good practice for you on Crystal. The competition will be a lot harder against the Pony Club competitors, so the Starlight gymkhana will be a great chance for you girls to prepare for that.'

Oh yes, Poppy knew. She might win all the games at the Starlight gymkhana, like her favourite bending and barrel racing competitions, but it was only practice for the big event a few weeks later.

Out of all of Sophie's pupils, Poppy knew she had the most experience, which is why she had always been given first pick of ponies. But riding in her age group at the big Pony Club competition would be a whole new experience, and she was going to have to put in hours of extra practice with Crystal if she wanted even a chance of winning a ribbon.

'Talking about the other girls,' said Sophie. 'We'd better get a move on. Mark only had a couple of hours off work to look after things while we rode, and they might already be here.'

CHAPTER THREE

New Friends

Poppy sat up in the saddle, alert, at the edge of the grass where the trail ended. Aunt Sophie brought Jupiter to a halt, and Poppy followed suit with Crystal, facing Starlight Stables. Two cars were parked near the stable block, which meant that the other girls were here. Poppy felt her stomach flutter, like it was full of butterflies. It was the same kind of nervous feeling she got before approaching a big jump on horseback – a mixture of excitement and nerves.

Poppy noticed that the cars weren't the usual big and expensive types that most of Sophie's pupils arrived in, which she was secretly pleased about; if the girls weren't fancypants horse riders, they were more likely to be like her and super excited about having their own pony.

'Looks as if we've got company,' Aunt Sophie said.

'Do you need me to do anything this morning? Like help out with the feeding or mucking out?' Poppy asked her, secretly wanting an excuse to escape and watch the girls from afar before meeting them.

'Since you and Crystal are doing so well, why don't you stay mounted for now? Mark and I can bring the ponies out for the girls to have a quick ride, and then you can take them for a trail ride, maybe.'

'Okay.' Poppy smiled, pleased she could keep riding Crystal.

Uncle Mark came out of the barn with two neatly turned-out ponies, both already saddled up. Sophie jumped to the ground and led Jupiter on foot the rest of the way back to the stables.

Poppy swallowed a lump in her throat and rode Crystal slowly behind her aunt. She was kind of scared about meeting the new girls. Aunt Sophie and Uncle Mark were counting on her getting along with the other girls, but what if they didn't like her or want to hang out with her?

'Poppy!' Uncle Mark's voice called out.

She rode closer to him, nudging Crystal to keep walking when she saw four adults come out of the barn. They must be the girls' parents, she realised. Her pony must have sensed her hesitation and thought she wanted her to halt. Poppy gave a feeble wave as all eyes turned on her. At almost the same time, two girls emerged from the barn, helmets on, whips in hand. One wore smart cream jodhpurs that looked as if they hadn't seen daylight before, let alone horses, and the other was in dark blue jods.

'Ah, hi,' Poppy stammered. It felt like her stomach was leaping up and down, over and over.

The other girls seemed every bit as nervous as she felt.

'Poppy, I'd like you to meet Amelia Walker and Katie Richards,' Uncle Mark said.

Poppy looked from one girl to the other, trying to figure out who was who. She was desperate to look over the two ponies, but she didn't want to seem rude.

The dark-haired girl in the cream jods giggled and rolled her eyes. 'I'm Milly,' she said, tucking a loose strand of curly brown hair behind her ear. She had freckles across her nose and she was the shorter of the two, and her grin showed off her braces.

The man she now realised was Milly's father groaned. He must have liked Amelia better. The other girl just smiled and said a quiet 'hello'. Her arms were crossed, like she was hugging herself.

Katie's parents looked rather reserved in comparison to the Walkers, but at least they were smiling. Katie's mum was like an older version of her, only her blonde hair was cut shoulder length while Katie's golden hair was braided in a fish plait.

'I've just showed *Milly*,' Uncle Mark said with a wink, 'and Katie their ponies. If all goes well today, then they'll be back here for the rest of the holidays, commencing at the end of the week.'

He beamed at the girls. But the moment was short-lived as the woman standing next to Milly's dad started speaking.

'I'm just not sure about Amelia staying for all that time. Is it really such a good idea?'

Milly glared at her parents. 'I've told you, Mum, I'm staying. It's the best thing that's happened to me, like, ever!'

Aunt Sophie arrived in the nick of time. Everyone liked Sophie – Poppy had seen firsthand how she always managed to calm parents down when their kids were riding.

'Hello there.' Her aunt had changed into a clean pair of jodhpurs and a crisp shirt, her hair swept up into a swishy ponytail. 'It's so good to see you all again. How are we, girls?'

Poppy watched as the parents all smiled back at her aunt, and, before they could start complaining again, Sophie had turned to the girls. 'How about I take you out to the arena and, Mark, you can give the Walkers and the Richards a proper tour of the farm. Do you have time before your rounds?'

'Sure thing.' Uncle Mark gave her a smile but flicked her on the shoulder on his way past, like the last thing he wanted was to be stuck with the parents. Poppy clamped her hand over her mouth to stifle a giggle and noticed that Katie had seen it, too.

With the parents and Uncle Mark gone, Aunt Sophie had hold of both the other girls' ponies and was focusing again on riding.

'Let's meet the four-legged friends,' she said.

That got all three girls' attention. Poppy stayed

mounted on Crystal, pleased that Milly had come to stand beside her and was stroking her pony's neck. All the horses were gorgeous, but Crystal had that something special, or at least she thought so.

'Okay, girls, this is Poppy's brand-new horse, Crystal. Crystal measures 14 hands high, and she's a Welsh/Arab cross.'

Aunt Sophie paused and Poppy tried not to smile too hard.

'Here we have Joe,' she continued, indicating toward the bigger of the two ponies she held. 'Joe is a full 14.2 hands high, and he can be a little cheeky sometimes, so he needs a firm hand. He was owned by a young friend of ours who has now outgrown him. She had a lot of fun on him.'

Poppy watched Joe, his ears pricked. He looked like a real character, with his slightly up-turned nose and white blaze.

'Any ideas of his breeding?' asked Aunt Sophie.

The three girls all looked at one another. Poppy bet the other two were as scared as her to get it wrong, and she bit down on her lip as she glanced quickly at first Milly then Katie.

Sophie looked between them all and continued,

not seeming to notice their nervousness. 'Joe is three-quarters Arab, so that's why he's fun and looks like trouble. All being well, he'll be Milly's horse.'

Milly dropped her whip and flung her arms around a startled Joe. Poppy thought they kind of suited each other, because Joe didn't even flinch.

'This here is Cody,' added Sophie, indicating for a still-shy Katie to come forward. 'As you can see, Cody is, a palomino, and he's the same height as Crystal at 14 hands. He's an English riding pony, and he's a very talented dressage and event mount.'

Katie moved forward tentatively and stood beside him. She didn't look scared, but she still didn't say much. Poppy watched as Cody sniffed her and then drooped his head down for a cuddle.

'Okay then, let's see you both up there for a ride. Let me know what you think, and if your pony is suited to you. Then maybe you girls could all head off for a bit of a ride around the farm and through the surrounding bush. What do you say, Poppy?'

'When have I ever said no to a ride?'

That earned her a nervous laugh from Katie and a big grin from Milly. Poppy was relieved they seemed to like her.

While Poppy sat on Crystal, watching the others in the arena, she realised how being back at the farm was making her feel like her old self again, like everything was okay. She still missed her dad all the time, and wished he could come home, but being with horses and riding Crystal made her feel so much better.

She hoped the girls were as nice as they seemed, because if there was one thing that could make her holiday better than ever, it would be having two new horse-crazy friends.

CHAPTER FOUR

Trail Riding

Crystal snorted and started to jig-jog – a sure sign she was ready to do something more exciting than walk. Poppy relaxed the reins and looked over at Katie and Milly who were riding alongside her. She realised something very worrying – she was going to have to up her game.

Ever since she'd started riding at Starlight, Poppy had been the best. There were older kids who had more experience, but everyone made a fuss of how good a rider Poppy was. She wasn't bothered about any other sports, partly because she hated the idea of having to do anything other than ride on the weekends. Horseriding was the one thing in the world she was really good at.

But Milly and Katie were easily as good as her, and they'd been especially chosen by her aunt and uncle as being worthy of a scholarship. Poppy felt the pang of jealousy again, but pushed it down – she would just have to prove to Aunt Sophie and Uncle Mark that she truly deserved her pony by trying extra hard to be the best.

'How do you know the Delaneys?' asked Katie.

Poppy snapped out of her daydream and turned to look at Katie. She was surprised by her question. She'd just presumed they knew.

'Ah, they're my aunt and uncle.'

Milly squawked and turned in the saddle. 'You're telling me that the one and only Sophie Delaney, like, one of the best dressage riders in the country, is your aunt?'

Poppy laughed. Well, when she put it like that, it did sound pretty cool.

'Yep, she's pretty amaz–'

Milly interrupted her. 'That's awesome! Do you live with them or something?'

Poppy noticed that Katie was watching her, too, like she was really interested in her answer but was too shy to ask. Poppy knew that she liked the girls already – even if they were a threat to her star-rider status – but she wasn't ready to talk to anyone about her mum or dad, about what had happened.

'My family just moved, so I haven't been out here for a while, but I usually come and stay here a lot,' she said instead.

Milly groaned, but Katie stayed quiet.

'You're so lucky to have them! My mum knows NOTHING about riding but thinks she's an expert, and my dad just wants me to work hard at school and forget about stupid horses.'

Poppy gave Milly a sympathetic look. Secretly, she was pleased Milly wanted to moan about her parents, because it meant she wouldn't have to talk about hers.

She waited for Milly to say something else, but she seemed done moaning about her parents, so Poppy quickly asked Katie a question, before Milly asked her anything else.

'What about you, Katie? What are yours like?'

Katie almost looked embarrassed. 'My parents are, well, kind of okay.'

Milly scoffed. 'No parents are okay!'

Poppy ignored her and waited. 'What do you mean?'

'They love that I like riding. The only problem is, we have no money, and I have three little brothers, and there just really isn't any time for me and horses any more. Before the twins were born, I had lessons every week.'

'At least they like horses, though, right?' Poppy pointed out.

That made Katie smile, even if she did look like she was going to burst into tears. 'Yeah, but if it wasn't for the Delaneys, I wouldn't even be able to ride again. My dad just told me that they can't afford to pay for my riding lessons any more. Not even once a month like I'd been having.' Her eyes welled up with tears, and she patted Cody nervously on the neck.

Milly leaned over and gave Katie's pony a pat on the neck, too, as they rode side by side.

'Enough doom and gloom,' Milly said with a smile. 'Let's do some exploring. This holiday is going to be about riding, riding and more riding! While we're here, we don't have to worry about anything, right?'

Poppy couldn't have put it better herself. She grinned and looked over at Katie, pleased to see she wasn't crying. She knew how hard it was to fight tears.

Instead, Katie smiled, double wattage. Milly seemed like heaps of fun, but Katie was pretty cool, too, Poppy thought. She bet that once they got to know each other she wouldn't be so quiet, either.

'Last one to jump that log's a rotten rat,' yelled Milly, taking off at top speed.

'No cantering!' Poppy called back, feeling nervous.

Milly pulled up to a halt, her horse's head up high, dancing on the spot. 'Don't be such a spoilsport!'

Katie looked at Poppy, and Poppy looked back. When Katie, who seemed to be the sensible one, shrugged and pushed Cody forward, Poppy gave up worrying. What harm could they do having a play through the trees and into the bush?

'Come on!' called Milly, taking off again.

Poppy and Katie dug their heels in and raced, too, over the dirt track and toward the little log. Milly took the jump first, then halted, puffing, on the other side. It was a wide jump, and Poppy and

Katie cleared it at the same time.

'Let's go!' ordered Milly.

They trotted off after her, ponies pulling on the reins as they tried to stay ahead of one another.

'What's over there?' asked Milly, pointing to a clearing with a rickety wooden gate.

Poppy pushed Crystal to go a little faster through the bush and out of the dense trees, to catch up with Milly. She followed Milly's finger across the bridle path, past the 'No Trespassing' sign to the parched yellow cattle fields beyond. She groaned and felt herself shudder.

'That's Old Man Smithy's place,' she said, slowing Crystal to a walk, then halting. 'He's real scary. I'm not allowed to ride near his property.'

Katie looked worried, but Poppy noticed that Milly was grinning.

'So what's he done to make him so scary?'

Poppy gulped. She hated even talking about him. The last time she'd seen him he'd almost scared her to death. She'd been riding along the boundary and he'd suddenly appeared, walking out of some bushes with a poor cow hogtied on the ground behind him.

'He's this big old guy, real creepy looking. No

teeth, hair all sticking on end. He's farmed out here for ages, but Aunt Sophie and Uncle Mark have always told me to stay out of his way.'

'Have they ever said why?' asked Katie.

Poppy shook her head. 'Nope, they don't really talk about him. But it's weird how all the other neighbours let us ride through their land on trail rides and stuff, but we can't go near his place. Sophie goes all quiet whenever I ask about him.'

Milly's face lit up and she directed Joe near the boundary fence on the edge of the forest.

'Look!' said Milly, edging Joe closer. 'There are hoof prints here, and then on the other side. So someone must go riding through there.'

Poppy shrugged, amazed that anyone would risk riding through Old Smithy's land.

'I reckon we should go exploring,' Milly said. 'And I reckon you should ask your aunt again just what's so bad about him.'

'Exploring? Over there?' As she stared at the farm, Poppy wasn't so sure she liked having such an adventurous new friend. She could see Old Smithy's falling-down barn in the distance, and the trees that had fallen in a storm last year and not been cleared.

'Yeah, over there.' Milly turned in her saddle and looked at the other two. 'What do you say?'

Katie and Poppy glanced at one another and then back at Milly.

'I don't think so,' said Poppy. But she kept looking at the hoof prints. Milly was right. Someone had been riding that way – and recently. Must have been someone new to the area who didn't know, she figured.

'Well, I'm going for a look,' Milly said, wide-eyed. 'Don't you want to know why the Delaneys are so strict about his place?'

Poppy *had* always wondered. What had Smithy done to make her aunt and uncle stay clear of him?

The rumble of a truck made her sit straighter in the saddle. Poppy looked at her new friends and realised they'd heard it, too.

'That's him,' said Poppy, her voice low. She knew the sound of his ute's rumbly sounding engine from when he'd driven off after surprising her, with the hogtied cow flung on the back of his ute.

Katie looked terrified, but Milly just smiled, her eyes trained on the boundary, where the rumble was coming from.

'Are you sure?'

Poppy waited. His beaten-up blue ute rolled down the hill, weaving in the distance as it came down a hill toward them. The girls had pulled up closer to the gate, out of the cover of the trees, which meant he'd definitely be able to see them!

'Yeah, I'm sure,' she replied.

It disappeared again behind the trees, and Poppy shifted nervously. She didn't want to draw his attention so that he saw them watching, not when she had such an uneasy feeling about him. And besides, she took her aunt and uncle's rules seriously.

'Come on,' said Katie, pushing up her sleeve to check her watch. 'We were meant to be back by now.'

Milly looked at her own watch and sighed. 'Yeah, let's go, my parents will probably send out a search party if we're even ten minutes late. And then not let me come back!'

Poppy turned Crystal around. 'We can spy on him some other time. Come on, I know a short cut back.'

She knew the trails like the back of her hand, despite them being like a maze in places. Poppy had explored the bush for years and loved to shortcut through the dense trees.

'Is this the right way?' asked Katie as Cody negotiated a tricky corner and she ducked just in time to avoid a low-hanging branch.

'Trust me, I've been riding through here since I was eight,' Poppy said, as she pointed Crystal towards an overgrown path that she knew would bring them out around the back of the farm's stables. A kookaburra flapped out of a tree and made her jump, but Crystal just snorted and trotted past, head held high.

Poppy was enjoying showing off her knowledge of the trails, even if her heart was in her throat from the bird appearing out of nowhere. She just hoped she hadn't told Milly too much about Old Smithy. Poppy got the feeling that Milly sought out mischief, and that made Poppy worry. Old Smithy was trouble, she just knew it, and she hoped that Milly would forget all about wanting to ride on his land...

CHAPTER FIVE

Let the Fun Begin

In all the years she'd been coming to Starlight Stables, Poppy had never tired of the holiday riding camps, even though they did the same thing each time. Each camp lasted a week, and the kids learned to canter and jump, as well as ride through water and care for the pony they rode. Her aunt spent a lot of time with the camp children and did most of the instructing herself, and she always checked on them at night, too, in the bunk rooms before leaving them with the night-time carers.

Uncle Mark and Aunt Sophie let Poppy come to the camps all the time, telling her she paid her own way by helping so much, which meant she'd never had to ask her mum or dad for the money.

Poppy stroked Crystal's face absent-mindedly, thinking how much she loved being here. She missed her friends, though, even more this time, especially Sarah after she'd spent so much time at her house when her dad died. She'd messaged Sarah earlier, but not heard anything back. Poppy wondered what she was doing while Poppy was away. Not having any fun without her, surely, Poppy laughed to herself.

A squeal reminded her she wasn't alone.

Poppy looked at the bunch of kids – one or two were close to her age, but they were mostly younger. The odd one probably loved horses as much as she did, but she had a feeling that most of them just came here for something to do over summer. Poppy was in charge of the littlies for the next hour, as the head camp instructor had the morning off, and she knew exactly what would keep them entertained.

'Who wants to do some painting?'

Six eager faces turned her way.

'Like, with a paintbrush?' one of them asked.

Poppy laughed. 'No, silly, with our hands!' It had been one of her favourite things to do when she was little, putting coloured handprints on the grey ponies. 'Follow me! Pony painting, this way.'

When Aunt Sophie came to take over, Poppy was elbow-deep in paint. Crystal was covered in yellow, blue, purple and red handprints, her lovely grey coat like a multicoloured jacket.

'Thanks, kid. Sorry about the pony.' Aunt Sophie gave her an appreciative smile and flapped her arms, rounding up the children.

Poppy just shrugged. She supposed, being twelve, she was too old to find this sort of thing fun, but she loved it anyway. Even if it did mean extra work. Crystal would definitely need a hose down and proper wash, and quick, before the smudged handprints became sun-baked on.

The kids all flocked together and chased after Sophie, who was scolding them for running. Poppy laughed and pulled a sugar cube from her pocket, passing it to Crystal. She always used her pocket money to buy a bag at the supermarket before she came to Starlight.

There were only two days until Milly and

Katie arrived back, and Poppy realised that she was looking forward to them being here. In fact, she was excited! Once they were here, they'd all be having lessons with her aunt together, and she couldn't wait to have friends to trail ride with, too.

'Poppy, the girls arrive tomorrow,' Sophie said as they sat around the dinner table.

'A-huh.' Poppy tried to sound relaxed.

'We were wondering if they should stay up at the house instead of down in the bunk rooms with the other camp kids.'

Poppy liked the sound of that idea. It would be weird for them to be down there with the holiday camp kids and her to be in the house. 'Yep, that sounds great.'

Sophie smiled and brushed her fingers over Poppy's shoulder as she passed.

Less than twelve hours and they would all be together. Poppy felt a flicker of worry, and hoped that everything went to plan. Would they get along okay, week after week? She hoped so, especially since they'd be sharing a room, too. Because, except for a few days at home in the middle, they were going to have three whole weeks together.

Poppy was outside the stables, with her arm around Casper as she stroked his fur. Katie stood a few feet away near her parents' car, and Poppy could tell that she was close to tears. Poppy watched as Katie's mum hugged her – the kind of big, tight hug that showed she really cared. Poppy stared at her boots and kicked the gravel, thinking how much she missed those kinds of hugs from her mum.

'You just call if you need me, okay?' Her mother looked on the verge of tears, too. 'We'll be out next week, so it's not long.'

Poppy saw Katie nod and rub her sleeve over her eyes, sniffing as her mum got into her car and drove away. Poppy went forward and picked up Katie's bags for her, giving her a soft nudge on the shoulder.

'You'll be fine,' she said, wishing she knew how to make Katie feel better.

Her new friend braved a shy smile back, blue eyes still swimming with tears. 'I know, it's just that I've never really stayed away from home before.'

Poppy understood that, sort of. She'd always loved coming to the farm and staying with Mark and Sophie, even if she did get homesick. Even now, being worried about her mum, she was still happy to be on the farm.

The crunch of gravel made them turn and see another car coming up the driveway toward the stables. Casper trotted over to the vehicle, his tail wagging.

'See ya.' Milly flung open the passenger door and launched herself out of the car before it had even stopped properly.

Her mother looked alarmed and braked hard, bringing the car to an abrupt stop, but Milly just gave her a wave, bag already over her shoulder. She didn't have much stuff with her.

'Hey, you two,' she said, a wide grin stretching her face, and a hand on Casper's thick fur as he wagged his tail and leaned against her.

Katie snuffled but smiled, and Poppy gave Milly a beamer back.

'You ready?' Milly said.

Poppy and Katie looked at one another.

'Ready for what?' asked Poppy.

'The best, most fantastic summer holiday of your life!'

Poppy found herself laughing as Milly thrust one hand out and shook her dark curls back over her shoulder. She hadn't seen her with her hair out before, and it looked pretty, if not a little wild.

'Who's with me?'

Poppy dropped Katie's bags and put out her hand to cover Milly's. 'Me!'

Katie seemed to forget about her tears and covered the top spot with her palm. 'Me, too.'

'Let the fun begin!' squealed Milly.

'Sorry to break up the party, girls, but we need to get the ground rules sorted this morning.' Aunt Sophie was leaning against the stable entrance, dressed in cream jodhpurs and a sleeveless pink shirt, her long blonde hair twisted into a fishtail braid. Tall leather boots completed her outfit, making her legs look unbelievably long. Poppy hoped she looked like that when she was older.

'Come on,' said Aunt Sophie. 'Follow me.'

CHAPTER SIX

Learning the Ropes

The three girls trooped after Aunt Sophie, through the stable block and past the horses, stopping at their ponies' stalls. There were only three ponies in – the rest were either out grazing or down in the yards by the camp. Usually it was only the bigger horses that spent time in the stables, unless one of Sophie's private pupils was keeping their pony at the farm, which made Poppy feel even more special, that Crystal, Cody and Joe were being kept here.

'Joe and Cody have been left in so you can take them out this morning yourselves,' Sophie explained. 'But usually, I let them out into the paddock before 8 a.m., unless we have a morning ride scheduled. We only do this for the horses and ponies being ridden each day. They then come in for their night feed, and spend the night stabled.'

The girls left their bags by the door, and Poppy giggled as Milly showered Joe's nose with kisses when he poked his head over the stall.

'Do we have to make up their feeds?' Milly asked.

'Whoa, slow down, I'll go through everything with you.' Aunt Sophie walked off down the middle of the stable block, and the girls scrambled to follow.

'The feed room is this way. Poppy can help you to start with. Each horse has their feed written up on the board, but it won't take you long to memorise. Once you know your chaff from your barley and pellets, it all becomes very simple, but make sure you follow my instructions. Too much grain for a pony like Joe could make him hot tempered and silly, and other ponies need more to keep weight on when they're in work and being ridden regularly.'

Aunt Sophie walked on, talking as she went.

'Tack shed is to the right – you all saw that the other day. Please keep your tack clean as there will be weekly inspections.'

Aunt Sophie stopped and Poppy watched the other two girls look around, bewildered expressions on their faces.

Sophie laughed. 'You two look terrified.'

Poppy had to agree. Even Milly had gone from plucky and yapping to quiet and shell-shocked. When they didn't answer, Sophie pulled up a feed bucket that had been left outside a stall and turned it over, then indicated for them to do the same. Poppy found another bucket and dropped down on it. Casper had followed them in and sat on her feet, and Poppy kissed his head and ran her hand down his back. He responded by thumping his tail so she kept stroking his fur.

'It probably seems like a whole lot to take in, but I really need all three of you to fend for yourselves and your horses here as much as you can.'

Poppy understood all this already. She'd had the same conversation with her aunt and uncle a couple of years back.

'With Mark buying the local vet practice and me training for the World Dressage Champs, time and money are hard to find,' explained Aunt Sophie, her blue eyes searching out each girl. 'For us to make the scholarships work, and to pay off your new ponies, we go without a full-time groom here, so that means you all need to chip in and help out where you can.'

No one said anything, and silence filled the stables. Poppy knew she should speak up, but she didn't know what to say. Had she been wrong in thinking the other two were like her? Happy to work hard in exchange for riding every day?

'I'm pleased to work here,' chirped up Milly, back to her usual self. 'It's just a lot to learn.'

'Yeah, me too,' added Katie.

Aunt Sophie looked at Poppy.

'You know I'll do anything to help,' said Poppy.

'Okay then, girls, let's have a quick run-down over the chores, and then Poppy can take you up to the house to settle in.'

'Sure thing, Mrs D,' said Milly, saluting her like an army cadet.

That sent them all into peals of laughter, Sophie included.

'You don't have to call me Mrs D,' she laughed. Poppy smiled as her aunt touched Milly's shoulder when she stood. 'I want you to think of me like your big sister while you're here. "Mrs D" sounds way too formal.'

Katie laughed and said it, too. 'Mrs D.'

Milly gave Aunt Sophie's plait a cheeky tug when she jumped up, which made them laugh all over again.

'It kinda suits you,' she said, and they all nodded.

Even Poppy had to agree with Milly that it was kind of cool. 'I think so, too.'

'Back to chores,' said Aunt Sophie, firmly, but she was still smiling. 'We've got a lot to get through.'

They all groaned, and Poppy dragged her feet as she stood and followed the others.

'Poppy will be in charge for the first few days, as she knows the drill,' Aunt Sophie said as they stood around her. 'The paddocks need to be mucked out, stalls cleaned, and there are riding school horses that need to be exercised. We have fifteen horses here to keep fit for the weekend riding lessons, although many of those are currently being used for the camp so it's a bit easier during the holidays. But in addition to your own pony and lessons, you will have to ride at least one other mount each day, once camp is over. Other days will be spent helping out with the summer camp kids for an hour or two.'

They had all gone quiet again, but this time Aunt Sophie didn't pause.

'Lessons will be held every second morning, alternating between dressage, jumping and games preparation. We'll also alternate theory and practical skills once a week.'

'Do we get time off to eat?'

Milly's question made Poppy giggle, but surprisingly her aunt kept a straight face.

'If you're good, meals will be provided.'

Katie looked worried, but Poppy jumped in.

'I've been doing the chores since I was eight. They're no big deal. And Aunt Sophie's no monster. She hardly even checks.'

'I don't check because you've never given me reason to, Poppy,' she reminded her sternly. 'Yet! So, any questions?'

Katie put her hand up. 'Are we only allowed to ride our pony every second day?' she asked.

'Good question. The lessons are to further develop your skills, but you girls can ride your own horses every day doing whatever you like. So long as you stay together, you can trail ride or hack out on the farm to your heart's content.'

They all smiled.

'Okay, class dismissed. Dinner is at seven every night, so just make sure you're finished up and back at the house before then.'

Milly nudged Poppy and whispered, as Sophie walked away, 'We're heading back there tomorrow.'

Poppy felt her stomach jump as Katie leaned in. 'Where?'

'You both know where. We're going to pay that Old Smithy guy a visit. I want to see what's so scary about him.'

Poppy gulped and Katie closed her eyes.

'Are you sure that's a good idea?' Poppy asked.

Milly grinned and picked up her bag. 'Mrs D said we could trail ride every other day. Who's even going to know?'

The girls all sat in Poppy's bedroom, Katie cross-legged on the floor and Milly curled up on Poppy's bed. Poppy stood with a wad of paper and a pencil in her hand, facing the other two. The room was usually spacious, but once they'd brought in the two stretchers for Milly and Katie to sleep on, there wasn't a lot of room left to move about.

'Okay, so who wants to go first?' Poppy asked.

Poppy decided that Milly only ever looked enthusiastic if what they were doing was either at high speed or involved excitement. Katie, on the other hand, looked alert and interested. It was only Milly who was goofing off and staring out the window toward the stables.

'What do we have to do again?' Milly moaned.

Poppy glared at her.

'For the hundredth time, Mrs D wants us to come up with three goals each,' explained Katie, her expression serious. 'We need them for our first lesson.'

Poppy chewed on the end of her pencil and thought hard. What did she want to accomplish this summer?

'Okay, I'll go first,' Poppy volunteered.

She passed the paper and pencil to Katie for her to jot down what she said.

'I want to be good enough to jump Crystal at a competition so I can enter the 60-centimetre show jumping class and win.'

'Yep, that's my first one, too,' Milly said, putting her hand up and nodding her head.

Katie glared at her. 'You can't just copy ours.'

Poppy couldn't be bothered with any arguing. She didn't care less if Milly copied.

'Number two,' Poppy continued. 'I want to learn to plait Crystal's mane and tail properly, so I can do it myself before competitions. And third... Well, I can't think of a third yet.'

Poppy took back the pencil and paper, ready to write down Katie's list.

'Okay, my turn,' Katie said. 'First, I want to learn to ride dressage properly.'

Milly groaned, so Poppy leaned across the bed and thumped her. She liked that Katie was into dressage. It was the hardest thing of all to do, and Aunt Sophie would love teaching her. Nothing could be more difficult than getting a horse to calmly obey commands in an arena, head on the bit, not to mention how difficult it would be to commit a dressage test to memory. Poppy had a hard time even remembering which letter was where around the dressage arena.

'Then I would like to learn how to ride a

cross-country course correctly, at the right pace. And lastly, I want to win the 60-centimetre show jumping at the gymkhana. Sorry, Poppy.'

Poppy just waved her hand. 'I don't mind if you win, I just want to get around it without falling off or knocking a rail!'

Poppy turned to look at Milly then, and she saw Katie do the same.

'What?' Milly asked.

'Your turn,' said Poppy, pencil poised.

'Okay, let me think…'

Poppy was just about to tease her about having nothing to say when the house phone rang. It was still on her bed from when she'd spoken to her mum, and its shrill noise made them all jump before Poppy picked it up.

'Hello, Poppy speaking.'

The voice on the other end belonged to a stranger. She'd thought for a second it might have been her mum calling back for some reason.

Poppy shrugged at Milly and Katie, and walked downstairs. 'Uncle Mark, it's for you,' she said, passing the phone over.

Aunt Sophie looked up from her book and smiled

as Poppy headed back to her room, but something made her stop on the stairs once she was out of view. Milly and Katie had walked out of the bedroom and were hanging over the banister of the stairs, chatting and looking down at her. Poppy planted her finger to her lips to get them to be quiet, realising something was going on by the tone of her uncle's voice. She tiptoed back down to the bottom step so she could listen, straining to hear what Uncle Mark was saying.

'Stolen? I can't believe it!'

There was silence. Poppy's heart was racing, but her body was frozen as she waited to hear more.

'Five coloured horses?'

Uncle Mark's voice was agitated, and when Poppy crept forward to look into the living room, she saw Aunt Sophie drop her book and start pacing the room.

'Yes, all right, we'll take all the necessary precautions,' Poppy overheard. 'If you need any assistance at all, please do call.'

Poppy bolted back up the stairs, eyes bulging.

'Stolen horses!' exclaimed Milly.

They all looked at one another. Milly and Katie looked as stunned as Poppy felt.

'Do you think our ponies will be okay?' asked Katie.

Poppy didn't answer. The only thing worse than not having a horse would be having one stolen.

'What does he mean by coloured?' asked Milly.

'You know, like pintos – brown and white,' said Poppy.

Footsteps alerted them to someone coming.

Poppy pointed toward the bedroom and they ran back in. Once there, they lay on their beds, doing their best to recap on goal setting so that anyone listening from outside would think they'd been there the whole time, and not eavesdropping from the stairs. Poppy jumped on her bed and the other two sat down on their stretchers.

A soft knock sounded on the door, and Sophie's blonde head peeped around it.

'Girls, there's something I need to talk to you about,' she said as she walked into the room and sat down on the bed next to Poppy.

The front door slammed and they heard heavy footfalls outside, walking across the gravel driveway.

Poppy, Milly and Katie all waited, eyes on Aunt Sophie.

'We just had a phone call from the police. It appears that there is a horse thief operating in the area.'

Katie looked terrified, but Poppy stayed calm.

'What do you mean?' Poppy asked, pretending like she hadn't heard any of the conversation downstairs.

'A number of horses from Brackenridge Stud have been taken. All the police have at this stage are some tyre tracks and a whole heap of hoof prints, but that doesn't give them any helpful clues.'

'Will our ponies be safe?' asked Milly.

Aunt Sophie sighed, her shoulders low.

'Mark is out now, padlocking the gates to both the main entrance and the working driveway that the tractors use. The stable block should be safe as it's so close to the house and we'd surely hear any activity.'

Poppy dug her nails into her palm as she listened. Her aunt's words were doing little to reassure her.

'Mark will move all the non-stabled horses into the paddocks close to the house, so we can keep an eye on them, too, and Casper will spend the night in the stables as guard dog.'

Poppy was even more worried about Casper

than she was about the horses. What if someone stole him? Her aunt and uncle's dog was almost as special to her as the horses!

'Will Casper be okay?' A shiver ran down Poppy's spine. 'Can't he stay in the house?'

'Poppy, he'll be absolutely fine. He'll be warm in there, and if anyone even gets close to the stable, his bark will wake us up. We wouldn't put him in the stables if we thought he wasn't safe.'

Sophie slung her arm around Poppy and gave her a squeeze, her eyes warm as she looked at each girl in turn.

'Safety has never been a problem here at Starlight, but I need all you girls to be extra careful now. No riding off the property alone, always stick together and keep your eyes open. If this thief thinks he's got away with it once, he might just try it again. But you don't have to be fearful. Just careful.'

With a sigh, Aunt Sophie rose and left the room.

Poppy was still taking in everything Sophie had just said when Milly leapt from her bed onto Poppy's.

'You know what this means?' she asked excitedly.

'Uh-oh,' groaned Poppy.

'Tomorrow, we're going to look for them. And we're starting at that creepy guy's farm.'

'What?' Poppy didn't know what she was more scared of; her pony being stolen or snooping around somewhere they shouldn't be.

'You saw the hoof marks. It could easily be the stolen horses,' said Milly.

'There could be lots of reasons for those hoof prints,' argued Katie. 'There must be heaps of horses all around here.'

'She's right. There are other riders who use the trails through the forest,' agreed Poppy. 'Riders on the other farms, and–'

'Yeah, but you said that no one's allowed to ride on Old Smithy's land,' Milly interrupted. 'Come on, Pops. There are some stolen horses, a weird guy over the fence, hoof prints going onto his land, and you're not even a bit suspicious?'

Milly made a good point, and Poppy couldn't help but agree with her. She was suspicious, but weren't they better leaving this up to the police?

'I think we should just wait and see,' she said.

Katie nodded. Milly didn't.

'This is our chance to save them!' Milly said,

flinging her arms out dramatically. 'Come on, just one look over there. One look.'

Poppy sighed and looked at Katie. She couldn't help but smile as Milly glared at them both.

'Okay, fine, but just one look, one time.'

Katie flopped face down into her pillow.

'Great,' said Milly, beaming from ear to ear. 'We're going to find those horses, I just know it. And if they're not there, then we'll just have to keep looking.'

What are we getting ourselves into, Poppy wondered. And how on earth was she going to stop Milly from doing anything stupid?

CHAPTER SEVEN

Trail Ride Trouble

Poppy knew they were up to no good. She'd never disobeyed her aunt before, and she couldn't stop the worrying thoughts from running through her mind as she got Crystal ready for their ride. She was also nervous about the horse thief, who could be lurking anywhere, waiting to steal their ponies.

'You girls have fun,' called Aunt Sophie as she rode Jupiter out from the stable block. 'And if you go on a trail ride, make sure you take a phone, okay?'

They all nodded and waved and went back to their ponies. Milly already had her saddle on Joe, but Poppy had only just finished grooming Crystal, and Katie was still brushing Cody.

'So, what's the plan?' Milly stood with her hands on her hips, waiting for them to answer. Today, her dark brown hair was divided into two plaits, and one was hanging over each shoulder.

Poppy and Katie gave one another the 'uh-oh' look. Even though they hadn't known each other for long, it was clear that Milly was trouble. With a capital 'T'.

'We're off on a trail ride, back by lunch?' Poppy tried.

Milly faked a yawn before turning her attention back to Joe.

Katie walked toward the tack room, and Poppy followed, needing to get her saddle and bridle. When she caught up with her new friend, Poppy saw that Katie looked as worried about their ride as she was.

'Are you okay about this?' Poppy hissed.

'Not really,' said Katie, glancing over her shoulder. 'Don't you think we should tell Mrs D what we're up to? I don't want to be sent home if they find out.'

Poppy shook her head. 'No way. She's always told me not to go near the place, so we can't tell her.'

'What other option do we have?' Katie said.

'Hu-hmmm!'

Poppy turned around and found Milly leaning in the doorframe. She looked mad as she stood twirling one of her plaits around her finger.

'Come on, guys,' she said. 'Where's your sense of adventure? We can go explore, have some fun and be back before anyone knows where we've been.'

The last thing Poppy wanted was to be the spoilsport, but she hated getting into trouble. What if Sophie did catch them? Would she send them all home? And how would her mum cope if Aunt Sophie had to phone and tell her...?

'You're not scared, Poppy, are you?' Milly said.

Poppy straightened her shoulders and narrowed her eyes. Scared? No, she was not. She didn't want to get into trouble but she wasn't scared.

'I'm in,' she said defiantly, even if deep down she wasn't that sure about the plan.

Katie looked bewildered. Out of them all, she was by far the meekest. She was pretty, sensible, a really good rider and certainly not a trouble seeker. Poppy was starting to think her summer would have been far less worrisome if it was just her and Katie.

'I just wanted to come here to ride, not get in any trouble,' Katie moaned.

Now Poppy stood next to Milly, watching Katie. She hated teaming up against her, but no one was going to call her a wimp. And, besides, it was kind of starting to sound like fun. If Milly wanted to investigate, then Poppy didn't really have a choice in the matter.

'What happened to "let the fun begin"?' demanded Milly, her hand outstretched.

Poppy shrugged and placed her hand over Milly's, sick of worrying. 'Come on, Katie. If it looks like trouble, we'll just ride back fast. I don't want to get into Sophie's bad books, either.'

Katie let out a deep sigh and shuffled over to Poppy and Milly, her hand limply resting on the other two.

'Let the fun begin,' she mumbled.

'Make it sound like you mean it,' said Milly. 'Let the fun begin!'

They all laughed.

Saddle in hand, bridle over her shoulder, Poppy followed Milly and Katie as they trooped back to the horses, saddled up and rode out to the trail.

There was only one other farm boundary to ride past after negotiating the first tight cluster of trees and bushes, and then they'd be there...

'So, have you ever actually seen Old Smithy up close?' asked Milly, pulling back on the reins to slow down Joe as they rode out onto the trail. 'Like, talked to him or anything?'

'Just that one time I already told you about, when he scared me as I was riding past. He was being really rough with this poor cow.' Poppy shuddered. She hated people being cruel to animals. 'Otherwise just from the car, or in the distance when we've been riding past,' Poppy answered.

'Do you think we need, like, a plan?' asked Katie, riding fast to catch up with Poppy and Milly. Cody, as usual, was behaving like a perfect gentleman, while the other two seemed jittery.

'Plan?' repeated Poppy.

'Yeah, like, a getaway plan if something goes wrong. Or maybe what our goal is once we get there.'

Milly bounced in the saddle, her excitement contagious.

'Yes! We do! Let's brainstorm.'

The girls all reined their ponies in and formed a half circle.

'There are two main things we have to think about,' continued Katie. 'We need an entry and an exit strategy, plus an emergency plan.'

Poppy grinned. Katie sounded like a grown-up sometimes because she was so sensible. 'See, this is why Katie is so valuable. You come up with the adventure stuff,' she said, pointing at Milly. 'I have the practical knowledge of the farm and bush trails, and Katie is like the genius mastermind.'

'So, then, Miss Planner, let's make a plan so we can do this already!' Milly clearly wasn't the best at sitting still. Poppy giggled as she watched her shift in the saddle, chomping at the bit to get going.

'Well,' said Katie, looking at Poppy. 'How do we get onto his land?'

'There's an old gate, about ten minutes ride from here. It's padlocked shut, but I reckon we could jump it. It's lower than the piece of fence we were looking over the other day.'

Katie was focused, her hands resting on Cody's wither. 'What about where we're going to ride to once we're on his land?'

'The big barn,' said Milly, her mischievous eyes glinting. 'I reckon we need to get inside it.'

Poppy gulped. That sounded way more dangerous than she'd been expecting. Did they really need to go into the barn?

'Inside?' Katie asked.

Milly waved her hand and made Cody jump. 'We'll see when we get there.'

Katie calmed her pony with a soothing hand to the neck. 'First, we need to practise jumping,' Katie said, 'so we can jump that gate and get in and out of Smithy's land as quickly as possible. And maybe we should come up with a noise that means danger.'

'Oooohhh, that sounds good. How about a horse noise, or a bird?' Milly said.

'Yeah, like an owl hoot or something. Like in the movies,' agreed Poppy.

'But I'm not up for the practice part,' moaned Milly. 'Let's just get going!'

Katie shook her head. 'We don't have to go back or anything, but don't you think we should go over the log in the track a few times? That gate will be bigger than anything I've jumped in a while.'

Poppy agreed. 'Yeah, imagine if we were chased off the land or something, and one of the horses wouldn't jump!'

That seemed to get Milly's attention. 'Okay, so who's up for a canter 'til we reach the fallen tree? We can go over it a few times, and then find this gate.'

'Let's go!' Poppy didn't feel as brave as she sounded, but she'd decided that it was about time she had some crazy fun. It seemed like she'd been covering up for her mum for so long that she was more like the parent than the kid. Now felt like as good a time as any to start being the kid again.

As the three girls rode Crystal, Cody and Joe along the track towards the old log, Poppy knew she was being naughty, especially when her aunt and uncle seldom gave her rules to obey. But she could hardly ruin the fun, could she? And besides, what was the worst that could happen? Even if Old Smithy did catch them, what could he do? If he was that dangerous, wouldn't Aunt Sophie have given her a reason for why they weren't allowed over there?

CHAPTER EIGHT

Old Man Smithy's

Crystal thundered along the track toward the fallen blue gum. Poppy focused on the parched trunk – the bark had all peeled off, making it almost pure white. Crystal cantered confidently and cleared the jump with ease. Poppy pulled Crystal up to the side of the log so they could watch the others take the jump. Joe was hot on Crystal's tail, zipping over the log and then pulling up to a halt from his canter. Cody approached gracefully and soared elegantly through the air.

'Okay, so practice done,' said a bossy Milly. 'This time, we're going over the real thing.'

Poppy's stomach churned nervously, but she didn't let it show. She was ready for this. She was on a fast pony and she was with her friends. She just had to tell herself that nothing was going to go wrong.

'Let's run through it one more time,' Katie said.

Poppy was amazed – Katie now looked even more confident than Milly. Poppy remembered hearing about that type of person: cool, calm and collected in the face of crisis, or something like that.

'I'm leader, you guys follow me,' said Milly.

'Fine, but I'm lookout,' said Poppy. She knew Milly was too set on adventure to pay attention to potential trouble. Best keep an eye on things myself, she thought. 'If I say go, we all get out of there – fast!'

'Good idea, Poppy,' said Katie. 'And so I'm in charge if there's an emergency. If we need to go, the lead falls on me, because Cody will always do as he's told. And I have the phone in case we need it, too.'

They all nodded their heads, pushed their heels down hard and gathered up their reins.

'Ready?' asked Poppy.

'Ready!' said the other two in reply.

Poppy watched Milly keep Joe at a steady canter. The trail stretched out to the left, but they were diverting off the trodden path and making for the old, rickety wooden gate with its rusted chain and padlock. The three horses fell back into a trot as low-hanging branches slowed their pace and scratched at the girls' bare arms.

'I'm just going to check it out first,' Milly called, riding on into the clearing ahead. 'Make sure it's safe on the other side.'

Poppy watched Milly trot toward the old gate and inspect the paddock.

'All clear,' Milly hollered, walking Joe around and riding back to Poppy and Katie.

Milly made Joe canter again, circling him on the grassy clearing before pointing him toward the jump. Poppy followed on at a safe distance, with Katie close behind her.

Poppy saw Joe pop over up ahead and land on the grassy field, only the slightest hesitation slowing him down. Crystal felt strong beneath her, eager to clear the fence and land with her friends on the other side. Poppy enjoyed the way her stride became slightly faster, pulling to get her head. Poppy held the reins firm, kept contact with the bit, and gave Crystal her head just as she took off from the ground.

Poppy hardly had time to think about how great they had jumped, though. The pounding of Cody's hooves behind made her move fast, and then it dawned on her exactly where they were. Old Man Smithy's place. Goosepimples ran down her arms and up the back of her neck. She needed to stay alert.

Cody cleared the jump with ease, too, and the girls were off. Milly signalled with her hand for them to ride straight for the big barn. It loomed within their sights. A big, dark building that was looking scarier by the second. The red paint was peeling from it and seemed almost brown it had faded so much. Poppy could see that the glass in one of the windows was broken, as if something had been thrown through with great force and left a hole right in the centre.

Katie moved up beside her, holding Cody in check as they headed toward the barn. There was a banging that startled Poppy, but it made her feel more sure about what they were doing, that the ponies could really be in there. Up ahead, Milly went faster still, sending them all into a cross-country gallop. Poppy even started to relax, her body softening from its rigid stance.

'Did you hear that?' she called out.

'Yes!' Milly called back at the same time as Katie.

Poppy leaned forward in the saddle, urging Crystal faster again, but then Milly was pulling Joe up hard, spinning him around almost on the spot, and yelling at them.

'Get back! Back to the bush!'

What? Poppy almost fell off she stopped Crystal so fast, yanking hard on her mouth. She was never usually rough with her hands, but Milly had scared the breath from her!

Katie didn't react quite so quickly, allowing Cody to turn in a more balanced circle, but she looked just as worried as Poppy felt.

And then Poppy saw it. The beat-up old truck was coming across the field, descending the low hill and approaching the barn. It was Old Smithy!

They raced back to the boundary jump, side by side, across the yellow grass. All three horses were lathered up in a sweat, galloping as quick as they could. Poppy's heart was racing, but she leaned low over her pony's neck, remembering to stay still in the saddle and focus. The last thing she needed right now was to panic and fall off.

'Slow down!' Poppy yelled, trying to make her voice heard in the wind.

They all steadied to a slow canter, falling back into position as they approached the old gate. Cody went first, popping over just like before, followed by Crystal and then Joe, who was fighting hard to get back into first place.

What would they have done if one of the ponies had stopped? He could have captured them, or worse! Poppy couldn't even think about it. A car horn tooted loudly and it sounded close, but no one dared look back. He'd seen them. And he was letting them know.

Once they were hidden by the tall trunks of the blue gums, they all slowed again. Poppy took the lead on Crystal, maintaining a fast trot.

'Keep going!' called Katie, her voice full of terror.

Poppy shook her head, just as scared as Katie, but thinking clearly now.

'We can't take the horses back blowing this hard,' Poppy explained, her voice unsteady. 'We need to cool them down a little, or Sophie will know something's up if she sees us.'

Milly broke into a canter and pulled up next to

Poppy. Her eyes were shining, and Poppy wondered if she had actually liked almost getting caught!

'Do you know any secret tracks back?' Milly asked. 'Like the one we took yesterday?'

Poppy thought for a second, catching her breath.

'Yeah,' she replied. 'Not secret, but kind of overgrown and tucked away.' At least this way Old Smithy wouldn't find them if he tried to follow.

Milly fell back and Poppy resumed her lead position. She couldn't help worrying that it had been her job to keep an eye out, and yet she hadn't seen anything. She had been so focused on riding, daydreaming about Crystal, that she'd forgotten how serious their quest had been.

They wound to the left and trotted over a small log in the track, but no one slowed. They were all too scared to even come back to a walk until the stables came into view. Their arms were scratched, the path was almost too narrow for horses to pass, and Poppy was beginning to wonder if they were on the right track. But Starlight Stables appeared like a safety net before them, and Poppy almost didn't care if they got in trouble. So long as they were all home safe. That was all that mattered.

CHAPTER NINE

Overnight Adventure

'Everyone heard the banging coming from the barn, right?' said Milly as they started to hose the ponies down. Even a vigorous brush down wouldn't get the thick sweat off their coats, and so they were hosing them first to clean and cool them.

Poppy nodded along with Katie, wondering if the others were thinking the same as her – that the banging sounded like hooves. They'd been almost silent since dismounting, and Poppy was certain the other two were still in shock, just like she was.

'The horse thief. It's got to be him, don't you think?' asked Katie as they entered the stables.

Poppy looked at Milly and nodded. They were

all in agreement. Old Smithy was the horse thief. But how were they going to prove it?

'What if he comes for our horses now that he's seen them?' Katie asked.

'I think we need to stay down here with them,' said Milly.

Poppy saw that she had that determined look on her face again.

'In the stables?' asked Poppy.

'Yes, in the stables. Who's with me?'

All three girls raised their hands.

'Let's give the ponies a quick scrape down to get the water off, and get them back to the paddock,' suggested Poppy. 'Hopefully, Sophie will never know anything's happened.'

Poppy pushed her bedroom door ajar and listened, her ears straining against the silence. The house was completely dark, and she could only just make out the sideboard on the landing as her eyes adjusted. The light was off in her aunt and uncle's room, but she wanted to make sure they were asleep. She heard Mark's whistley snore and relaxed.

'Is the coast clear?' whispered Milly.

Katie and Milly were behind her, sleeping-bags under their arms. They had been waiting for over an hour for Sophie and Mark to go to bed, but it had seemed like forever.

'I think so,' Poppy whispered back. 'Just follow me, and try to avoid the creaky steps.'

The old farmhouse was full of noisy floorboards but, after years of staying over, Poppy knew where most of the squeaky spots were. She pushed the door open enough to fit through, and stopped to check she could still hear her uncle snoring. She waved for the others to follow her, and walked into the hall. They headed for the stairs on tiptoes. Poppy carefully stepped over the stair that she knew to avoid, and winced when it squeaked behind her, sounding deafeningly loud in the silent house.

Poppy turned around and glared at Milly, and could just make out her friend mouthing a silent 'sorry' in the darkness. Poppy had a torch in one hand, and she switched it on once they had all got safely out the front door.

'They might see the light if we use it close to the house,' whispered Katie.

'How will we find our way then?' Poppy asked.

'Let's just link arms and go slowly. Once we're down the drive, we can switch it on,' said Milly.

'What if Casper starts to bark when he hears us on the gravel?' Katie asked.

'We'll call out to him before we get there, so he knows it's us. He's probably sound asleep anyway,' said Poppy. She could just make out the outline of the barn in the darkness ahead of them. Milly and Katie were either side of her, and she felt them pulling her gently forward, eager to get to the barn as quickly as possible.

All around them, unidentifiable objects lurked like creatures waiting to get them. Trees that were pretty in the daytime loomed like haunted skeletons in the dark, swaying ominously.

'Geez, I've never been so scared here,' muttered Poppy.

Katie squeezed her arm tighter, her voice soft. 'Me neither.'

The big stable block looked almost as scary as the trees, just because it was so big and dark. Poppy would never have walked out here alone in the pitch black without her new friends.

'Casper,' Poppy called softly. 'Hey, boy, it's just us.'

She turned the big handle and tugged the door until it slid open, then heaved it across as quietly as she could. Casper was waiting with his tail wagging.

'Woof!'

'Shhhhhhh,' they all hissed.

His bark had echoed but they all jumped on top of him. Showering them with licks, Casper wriggled, but didn't bark again, loving the attention.

The girls yanked the door shut and secured the latch, before sprinting over to check the stalls. Poppy raced to a very surprised Crystal. She was standing, happily munching her hay, startled only by the fact that the light from the torch had been swung directly into her face.

'Hey, girl.'

Poppy shone the light on the ceiling instead and reached a hand out to her. Crystal nuzzled it before turning her attention back to the hay.

Phew! Poppy had been so worried about Crystal, it had been all she could think about. She walked down to check on Jupiter next, who was snoozing, and then back to Milly and Katie.

'Do you think we'll get any sleep?' she asked.

Katie shook her head. 'I'm way too scared to sleep.'

'Me too,' Poppy said.

Milly was the only one who looked confident. 'Who needs sleep when we're protecting our horses?'

'Maybe we should do, like, a roster,' suggested Poppy, ignoring Milly.

Katie and Milly looked back at her with blank looks on their faces.

'We each take turns at keeping watch, so we can get some sleep and make sure everything is okay.'

'Sounds like a good plan,' Katie said, sitting cross-legged on the concrete floor, stroking Casper.

Poppy slumped outside Crystal's stall after she'd checked the other horses. She was feeling exhausted. The only thing keeping her going was the excitement of what they were doing, but that was starting to wear off, and she could feel her eyelids getting heavier and heavier. Crystal hung her head out every now and then to watch her, no doubt wondering what all the fuss was about. Milly and Katie sat almost opposite her, on guard outside Joe's and Cody's stables.

'You think we're safe out here?' Katie's voice broke the silence.

'No,' moaned Poppy, her eyes half-closed. 'But what other option do we have?'

'Have you set the alarm yet?' asked Milly. 'We have to be back inside by 6 a.m., when the Ds wake up.'

'Couldn't we just go back now?' whimpered Katie.

'No!' Poppy and Milly exclaimed together.

'I've waited years to get my own horse,' said Poppy. 'There's no way I'm going to let anyone steal her, or even get near her.' Because without her horse, she'd feel like she had nothing in her life to look forward to again. Coming here was one thing, but thinking about a holiday without Crystal? She didn't know how she could ever go back to not having her.

They sat in silence, huddled in sleeping-bags but still cold. Poppy wasn't enjoying this any more than the others, but what she'd said was true. There was no way anyone was going to take Crystal from her. Ever.

CHAPTER TEN

Uncle Mark to the Rescue

'Heels down, Poppy, and keep your eyes ahead,' called Aunt Sophie.

Poppy tried to concentrate, but her eyes would hardly stay open, let alone face forward.

'Katie, come on! Push him on.'

They all trotted around the arena, trying their best, but they were a mess, Poppy knew.

'Into the middle, now!' barked Sophie.

Crystal, Cody and Joe all turned in when the girls told them to, halting in the middle.

'Come on, girls. What's happening out there today? You can all do so much better.'

Milly yawned, Katie looked guilty, and so Sophie

looked to Poppy for an answer. Poppy struggled with what to say. She'd never been any good at lying.

'We didn't get much sleep last night,' she finally mumbled.

'What do you mean? You girls were in bed before nine o'clock.'

That made them all look at the ground.

'No secrets, girls. What's going on?'

Poppy was surprised when Milly spoke up first. 'We kind of spent the night in the stables.'

'We were worried about the ponies, you know, with the horse thief on the loose,' chimed in Poppy. She wanted to make her aunt understand, hoping that would make her less mad at them.

But Aunt Sophie glared at them.

'You mean to say you snuck out once Mark and I were asleep?'

They all nodded.

She at least smiled at them then, shaking her head. Now she looked more amused than angry. 'Well, I understand, but it was wrong to lie. We would have taken air beds down had we known you were that worried.'

'So you're not mad?' asked Katie.

'No, girls, I'm not mad, but you're still in trouble for not being honest with me. I do remember what it was like to love a pony as each of you do, but I'm also responsible for your safety while you're here, and I promised your parents that I would look after you.'

Milly's head snapped back and Poppy's eyes opened a little wider.

'Punishment?' she asked.

'See those cavaletti over there?' Aunt Sophie pointed.

Poppy and the others looked to where she was indicating. A row of six small cross jumps, set in a line. When they all looked back to her, she smiled and continued.

'No stirrups or reins. Today we are going to make sure you all have nice deep jumping seats. Knot your reins and let them go as you approach the jump, grip with your knees, arms out wide, bending at the hips. We're going to practise until you can do it with your eyes shut.'

Poppy, Milly and Katie all groaned, but Aunt Sophie wasn't taking no for an answer. Poppy knew that by the end of the day, her legs were going to ache so bad she would hardly be able to feel them. Going without reins was one thing, but riding without stirrups? It was torture, especially jumping. By the time they crawled into bed tonight their bodies would be beyond sore.

'Knot your reins and cross your stirrups now, and start a circle. Poppy, you're first. I want a nice balanced canter, and then keep going round and over the cavaletti until I tell you to stop.'

That night, the girls sat around the table, exhausted. They had hardly said a word since sitting down. Poppy was used to Sophie pushing her hard, but even she was feeling the pain this evening. At least having Milly and Katie here meant she had help with chores. Her muscles ached so much, she didn't think she'd have got through them without their help.

Poppy suddenly felt a kick under the table.

'Ouch!' She glowered at Milly, who was sat next to her. But Milly was holding her head funny.

Aunt Sophie and Uncle Mark looked their way.

'Sorry,' Poppy muttered. 'My legs are just sore from riding.'

But they hardly gave the girls a second look, going back to their conversation.

Poppy had no idea what was going on, or why Milly had felt the need to kick her. She was rubbing her leg when Katie bent in close.

'I think she wants you to listen to Mr and Mrs D,' she whispered.

Poppy quickly tuned in to her uncle's and aunt's voices. It wasn't like it was hard to hear them, she just hadn't bothered to listen.

'We're going to have to padlock the paddock gates, too,' Mark said. 'The fact that it's happened again means we could easily be next.'

That got her attention. More horses had been stolen?

'The worse thing is not knowing what happened to those horses. They could have ended up anywhere! How many went this time?' Aunt Sophie asked, her voice getting quieter.

Poppy kicked Milly back. This was interesting.

'Only two, from a roadside paddock. But still no clues for the police.'

'Ah, Mrs D, can I ask you something?' asked Milly.

'Sure.' Aunt Sophie wasn't even looking their way.

'It's just that Poppy said we can't ride on the farmland adjoining the trail. What did you say his name was, Pop?'

Poppy felt her eyes bulge. Why would Milly ask them that? Why would she even want to bring up the subject? Did she want them to know what they'd been doing?

Aunt Sophie looked down, and Poppy found herself wondering again what Old Smithy could have done to upset her aunt that much.

'I don't want to discuss him, Milly,' Uncle Mark said. 'But he's a horrible and dangerous man, and I don't want you girls going near him or his land, understood? He does a lot of hunting on his land, too – shoots rabbits, that sort of thing – and so it's not safe to be riding there in case of stray bullets, or the loud shots could spook the horses. And… I just don't trust him.'

'It's just that there were hoof prints near the boundary, so I thought maybe Poppy had got it wrong.' Milly's voice was sweet as pie, but it still made a cool shiver go down Poppy's back. 'Poppy sounded scared of him and I wondered why.'

Poppy watched as her aunt and uncle exchanged looks.

'Poppy was right,' Aunt Sophie said. 'No one from Starlight goes riding there, so don't even think about it.'

Uncle Mark cleared his throat and shook his head when her aunt touched his arm. 'Tell them,' he said, his voice low.

She sighed and looked at Poppy. Poppy blinked back at her, scared of what she was about to hear.

'Mark was witness to Smithy breaking another man's jaw in an argument outside a bar once, and if you'd seen the state of some of his animals in the past...' Her aunt pressed her palm into her forehead and stopped talking. 'We've made complaints before to animal welfare, so our relationship with him isn't exactly good. When we say we don't want you girls going near him, we mean it.'

Poppy couldn't breathe, she was so scared. So her aunt hadn't been exaggerating when she'd told her the old man was dangerous.

'Are we clear, girls?' Aunt Sophie asked.

Poppy nodded and watched her friends do the

same. Even Milly was quiet for once. Poppy got up from the table then and took her plate into the kitchen. She was sick to her stomach. Her aunt and uncle had gone back to their own conversation, and Milly and Katie followed her into the kitchen. They formed a quick huddle.

'We have to stay with the horses again tonight,' Poppy said, not wanting to leave Crystal unguarded for even a moment, even if she was beyond terrified of their neighbour now.

Milly looked at each of them, her eyes sparkling. 'You know what this means?' she said.

Poppy groaned, knowing exactly what Milly meant. But no way was she going to risk snooping around on Old Smithy's land again. It was too dangerous. 'Didn't you hear what they said, Milly? What if he thinks we're wild animals or something? What about what Mark saw him do that night?'

'We're going looking for the horses again tomorrow, and we're starting at that creepy guy's farm. We just need to be a bit smarter about it this time.' Milly was determined.

Poppy sighed and looked at Katie, who was staying very quiet. Poppy doubted Katie would ever want to go over there again either.

'The hoof prints do kind of make me wonder still,' said Poppy, thinking out loud. 'And the fact that we heard noises from inside that old barn. '

'You bet!' said Milly.

But before Poppy could say anything else, like how that didn't mean she was willing to risk running into Old Smithy again, Uncle Mark's deep voice made them all jump.

'What's going on, girls?'

'Ah, nothing, Mr D,' said Milly, giving him a beamer of a smile. Poppy was amazed at how Milly could just turn on the innocent charm like that. She and Katie probably looked guilty, but Milly's little act had given them time to compose themselves.

'Sounds like something's up,' he said, not missing a beat, and eyeing Poppy and Katie suspiciously.

Poppy felt her cheeks blush under his stare.

Aunt Sophie entered the kitchen then, sizing them all up.

'I'd say they're deciding whether or not to sleep down at the stables tonight,' she said.

'Stables?' Mark looked confused. 'Am I missing something here? Girls...?'

'Seems they've taken it upon themselves to guard their ponies. Are you planning on heading down again tonight?' Aunt Sophie asked.

They all nodded.

'Okay, well, let's get some bedding for you.'

'No, don't worry, Mrs D,' said Milly, linking arms with Poppy and Katie. 'We're fine on the straw in the spare stall. We'll just take our sleeping-bags.'

'Suit yourselves.' She sighed. 'Keep the cordless phone with you. If anything happens, call the house straightaway. And make sure the doors are locked.'

Poppy and the others scurried off upstairs then, before Sophie and Mark could change their minds.

'Why did you say no to the beds?' moaned Katie as soon as they were in the bedroom.

'Duh,' said Milly. 'We need to get to the stables now and start planning for tomorrow. No time for beds being lugged about!'

Poppy didn't say anything, but she had to agree with Katie. Her back and legs were aching, half from the jumping this afternoon and half from the bad sleep, or no sleep, last night. She would have done anything to sleep in a bed tonight, or at least on an air bed, but it clearly wasn't meant to be.

The phone rang then outside their room, and Poppy jumped. Ever since they had been almost caught by the truck the day before, she was terrified a certain someone was going to call and complain. And that was all they needed.

Poppy huddled closer to Milly and Katie, each of them tucked up in sleeping-bags. The odd nicker of a horse alerted them to the fact that they were most definitely not alone, but that didn't stop Poppy from feeling scared.

'Do you think we're safe here?' asked Katie, repeating her question from the previous night.

No, we're not safe, thought Poppy. There's a horse thief out there on the loose, a crazy old man who possibly is that thief on the next farm, and the only protection we have is a sleeping dog who is snoring so loud he isn't going to hear a thing!

'Yeah, we've got Casper,' she lied, looking over at the sleeping lump of fur on a pile of horse covers. 'No one could get close to the place without him knowing.'

Looking at the dog, Katie seemed less than

convinced. Milly, on the other hand, didn't seem a bit worried.

'Okay, so the first time didn't go down so well, but can you imagine when we actually find the stolen horses? We'll be famous around here!'

A loud bang made them all jump. Poppy almost screamed, but her tongue got in the way, and it sounded more like a duck quacking.

'Did you hear that?' whispered Katie.

'Why are we whispering?' asked Milly.

A thud followed by heavy footsteps made them all jump again, their three sleeping-bag bodies almost on top of one another. Poppy struggled to sit up and get to Casper.

'Casper!' Poppy shrieked. 'Casper, wake up!'

The dog raised his head, tail thumping. Next thing, the door handle rattled before being flung open. Poppy felt her heart pumping hard in her chest, and all three girls screamed as a large man was silhouetted in the doorway.

'Hey!' The dark silhouette in the doorway was suddenly illuminated, and Poppy saw it was Mark who stood under the light. 'What's with the screaming?'

Poppy slithered to the ground in a heap. She had never been so terrified.

'Uncle Mark! We thought you were the thief.'

Katie looked as white as a sheet, but Milly bounced forward, clearly interested in what Mark was holding.

'Hungry, anyone?'

That got Casper's attention. He leapt from his makeshift bed and sat to attention.

'Yes, bud, you get something for being a good guard dog.'

'Guard dog?' Poppy had never heard anything so funny. To think she'd been worried about big brave Casper being down here at night. He would probably sleep straight through all their ponies being stolen!

Uncle Mark emptied a bag of goodies onto an overturned bucket. 'Potato chips, Tim Tams and some lemonade to wash it all down,' he said. 'And I even have three raspberry lamingtons in here that I was going to give you for dessert tomorrow.'

'You're the best, Mr D.' Katie had come back to life.

'Thanks, Uncle Mark,' chimed Poppy. He

really was the best. She hadn't seen a lot of her dad growing up, but he'd been the same as Mark, kind and easy going, never upset by anything and always smiling.

'You girls need to remember to lock the door this time. Then, if someone does come snooping around, they won't be able to get in. Promise?'

Poppy gulped, her mouth full of soft lamington. Promise? How could they have forgotten in the first place?

He gave them a final wave and disappeared. Poppy jumped up to turn the lock and then shuffled back to the others, trying not to get tangled in her sleeping-bag, while licking her sticky fingers.

'They're pretty cool, huh?' said Milly.

'Who?'

'Your aunt and uncle.'

'Um, yeah, I guess.' They were, it was just that, sometimes, being with her uncle made her think too much about her dad, and then she started missing him all over again.

'Poppy, what's wrong?' Katie shuffled closer. She was sipping her lemonade, eyes wide with concern.

Poppy sighed. She'd only ever talked about what

it was like for her at home with her best friend, but she'd known Sarah for such a long time and so that had seemed okay. But then not telling Milly and Katie seemed wrong, too, because even though they hadn't known each other more than a week, she felt like she could trust them. She bet if Sarah was here, she'd be nudging her and telling her just to explain to them what had happened.

'They are your aunt and uncle, right?' Milly asked, grinning.

'Of course. It's just, well, this year has kind of sucked.'

Milly passed her the packet of Tim Tams and she pulled one of the chocolate biscuits out. 'What happened?' Milly asked.

Katie was waiting, too, watching her. Poppy sipped at her Sprite and took a deep breath. 'My dad was in the army and… he died a few months ago.'

Katie and Milly both stopped eating, frozen mid-bite, and stared at Poppy. Poppy's cheeks burned because she was embarrassed and wished she'd never said anything. She was about to cry, but she had to keep telling them now because otherwise she'd definitely cry and she didn't want that to happen.

'We had to move house, and it's been really hard on my mum, so I've kind of had to look after my little brother a lot.'

Milly still wasn't saying anything. It was probably the first time Poppy had known her to be quiet, but Katie sprang into action. She put her drink down and threw her arms around Poppy, hugging her so tight that Poppy couldn't move.

'That's the worst thing I've ever heard,' Katie said, keeping an arm around Poppy's shoulder.

'I'm really sorry, Poppy. I wouldn't have moaned about my parents if I'd known.' Milly looked embarrassed.

'It's fine, really.' Poppy smiled, trying to be brave. 'The hardest thing is seeing my mum sad all the time, because I hadn't seen my dad in so long anyway.'

She looked around the barn, wishing she knew what to say to change the subject. Then she spied Casper. 'He snores so loud, don't you think?' she asked.

Katie laughed, smiling at her like she understood Poppy was trying to change the subject. 'Yeah. Hey, so, where are we sleeping tonight?' asked Katie.

'I'm so tired after all that riding.'

Poppy looked about. There was a clean stall with fresh straw laid out, and it looked pretty inviting. She was pleased Katie had realised she didn't want to talk any more, too.

'How about in there?' she pointed.

Poppy grabbed the packet of biscuits and trudged off with the others, exhausted. Casper followed and made a bed in the straw beside them. Horse thief or not, they were all too tired to stay awake.

CHAPTER ELEVEN

Pony Detectives

Poppy fought to keep her eyes open. Everything seemed a blur, and she couldn't remember ever feeling this exhausted before. Every time she lifted the shovel it seemed to weigh double what it had the day before. Crystal's stall was clean, but she still had two more to go.

She glanced over her shoulder and caught sight of their makeshift hay bed from last night. It had felt like they'd only just fallen asleep when the kookaburras started laughing loudly in the trees around the stables, waking the three girls and announcing it was time to head back to the house to have breakfast and get dressed. Poppy yawned, remembering how she'd just wanted to pull her sleeping-bag over her head and go back to sleep. In fact, she still wanted to do that!

Taking a rest, pressed up against the wall, Katie looked just as tired as Poppy felt, her arms limp at her sides. Annoyingly, Milly was still perky. She seemed to need no sleep, had endless amounts of energy and dreamed up a million ideas to get them in trouble every spare minute she had.

'Yoo-hoo. You girls in there?' Aunt Sophie's voice echoed through the stables, and Poppy straightened her shoulders, blinking fiercely. If her aunt saw how exhausted they were, she would probably call an end to their nights in the stables. And then who would protect their ponies? Although Poppy actually had no idea what they'd do if someone did try to steal them.

'Hi, Mrs D,' called Milly.

Katie managed a smile, and Poppy dropped the shovel onto the wheelbarrow.

'Morning,' Poppy replied.

Sophie stopped for a second and then walked down to Jupiter's stall. The big gelding hung his head over the half-door and nuzzled Sophie's hair.

'This morning, I'd like you all to saddle up and come watch me work Jupiter in the arena. I'm going to teach you a new dressage move, then we'll go for a ride to the other side of the farm.'

Poppy stole a look at Milly. Milly would be annoyed, but there was nothing they could do.

'Do you mean we're having a lesson today instead of tomorrow?' asked Katie.

Today was supposed to be the day they went back to Old Smithy's farm. Could they even wait until the next day? What if Mr Creepy came looking for them before they'd had a chance to prove he's the horse thief? Surely it wouldn't be that hard for him to figure out that they were from Starlight Stables. It was pretty much the only place around here where there were young girls on ponies!

'Exactly,' said Sophie, letting herself into Jupiter's stall. 'I have the farrier coming tomorrow, so we're having a change around.'

Poppy started to push the barrow. That set the other two back to task, leaving Sophie to lead her horse out and cross tie him outside his stall.

'Meet me out front in fifteen minutes.'

'Come on, guys,' whispered Poppy.

Once they were all out of earshot she stopped pushing. 'It's no big deal. Another day isn't going to change anything.'

'What about the farrier? Doesn't that mean Mrs D will be hanging around the stables instead of spending all day with the camp kids?'

Poppy shook her head. 'It doesn't matter. We can just tell her we're off on a trail ride.'

She knew it was kind of weird that, up until yesterday, she'd been dead scared of riding back to Smithy's place whereas now she was excited. But there was just something about knowing those stolen horses could be locked inside that big barn that was nagging at her. She wanted to get to the bottom of it and, for the first time ever, she didn't mind if it meant getting in trouble. Horses were the most important thing in her life, and she bet her aunt would have done anything to save a horse when she was a pony-mad kid, too!

'If you watch where Jupiter's head is, you'll see that he is perfectly on the bit.'

Poppy nodded. It didn't matter how many times

she watched the huge horse perform dressage, she was always mesmerised by how he and Aunt Sophie looked like they were floating. Jupiter's strong legs lifted and fell gracefully, his whole body arched, and Aunt Sophie seemed to move in perfect harmony with him, even at the sitting trot. Poppy knew from experience that sitting still at the trot was easy to watch but incredibly hard to master.

'She is awesome!' said Katie, like she'd never been so impressed with anything in her life.

Even Milly, who usually goofed off after sitting still for too long, was watching.

'Jupiter is a pro at this now, but it wasn't always this simple,' explained Aunt Sophie as she slowed him to a walk. 'What I want you girls to do is get in a habit of asking your pony to be on the bit whenever he's in the arena. When you're out trail riding or having fun, just enjoy yourself, but when you're in here, make them take riding seriously.'

'What if they won't stay on the bit?' asked Katie.

Poppy nodded her head. It wasn't exactly easy.

'That's what we're going to practise. You don't need to do it all the time, it takes a lot of effort to accomplish, but I want you to try your best.'

She pushed Jupiter back into a working trot, and they watched as his head stayed down, still arched, even when she asked him to canter. Then he came to a dead halt. Miraculously, his head was still lowered perfectly.

'Okay, girls. Check your girths, and then enter the arena. Start a 20-metre circle at the walk.'

They did as they were told.

'I need you all to shorten your reins slightly. Maintain a firm but gentle contact with the bit.'

Aunt Sophie was watching them closely. Poppy could feel eyes on her. She sat as straight as she could, pushing her heels down firmly. She loved that they were doing dressage practice, even if it was hard.

'Now, I want you to keep an elastic contact with your outside hand. Hold the rein on the outside steady, with no movement. Once you have done this, I want you to move your inside rein away from your pony, toward me. You will need to squeeze with this hand, and then give, repeatedly, for your pony to accept the bit. I want those hands as soft as marshmallow when your ponies respond, and lucky for you girls, they do know what you're asking, so it's not like we're teaching them something they haven't done before.'

Poppy was struggling to remember everything to do. It didn't sound like much, but keeping heels down, back straight and doing something different with each hand wasn't exactly easy.

'As soon as your pony responds, you are to make the softest contact possible with that inside hand. Soft hands are your reward to your pony for listening. It also encourages them to bend in toward the centre slightly. Whenever they're on the bit and behaving, you're to keep the contact very gentle.'

'Like this?' called Katie.

'Excellent!' Sophie replied. 'The trick is to respond instantly. Horses appreciate soft hands from their rider, so as soon as they learn that head down equals gentle, it will all become easier. And because your ponies know what's expected of them, it's simply a matter of you girls catching up to them, showing them that you understand, too.'

'Joe's not listening,' complained an impatient Milly.

'Stay calm, Milly, and listen to your pony. Joe's trying to respond, but you're giving him mixed signals. When he so much as puts his head down slightly, reward him by softening. Be firm when you ask and immediately soft when he accepts.'

Poppy could hear what was being said but she was focused on her own riding. Crystal was trying hard, and she was responding as quickly as possible. She did have a slight advantage, though, having watched Aunt Sophie train for so many years, seeing every dressage move she tried. Poppy was also desperate to be the best rider, to impress her aunt. Receiving praise from Aunt Sophie was one of the best feelings in the world.

'Great work, Poppy!' Aunt Sophie's voice boomed out, and Poppy felt exhilarated. 'Milly, Katie, pull up beside me in the centre. Poppy, keep riding. I want you to do exactly what you are doing now, but push Crystal into a trot. Remember also to keep your inside leg on if she tries to make the circle smaller. She's listening to your hands *and* your legs.'

Poppy squeezed her legs and Crystal responded by trotting, but her head popped up as soon as they were going faster. Poppy remembered Sophie's words and stayed calm, asking with her inside hand, slowing her movements as she rose to the trot. Like clockwork, Crystal's head went down, her neck rounded, and Poppy rewarded her by softening contact.

A clapping noise made Poppy's head rise, and she came back to reality. It was her aunt.

'Well done, Poppy. Bring her in.'

Poppy felt her cheeks flush, but she was proud. Milly's and Katie's enthusiastic clapping told her they were proud of her, too.

Crystal truly was a star.

The field stretched out in front of them. Long, yellowy green grass, as far as the eye could see. Crystal trotted forward, fast enough to make a breeze blow across Poppy's face. Poppy was nervous, though, as they rode along beside Sophie. There was a tiny possibility that they might see the scary neighbour once they reached the blue gums in the distance. But that was being silly. They were still on her aunt and uncle's farm, which meant she should feel safe.

Grazing near the boundary, a herd of dairy cows caught Poppy's attention. It struck her that they looked awfully like coloured horses.

'I thought we'd go for a canter down the west side of the farm, and then let the horses have a splash in the creek.' Sophie's suggestion interrupted Poppy's train of thought, but she smiled as Milly and Katie whooped at the idea.

'Ever been swimming with a horse before?' Sophie asked.

Milly and Katie both shook their heads, and Sophie winked at Poppy.

'Well then, let's teach these two how to swim!'

Going to the creek meant heading toward the opposite boundary, so swimming sounded good to Poppy, too. She almost forgot about the trouble they were set to make tomorrow in her excitement to get to the water.

'Okay, no faster than a nice canter. Just call out if you want to stop,' instructed Sophie.

Jupiter went first, his long stride eating up the ground. Poppy and the other two spread out to her left, forming a straight line, but they had to go fast to keep up.

'All okay?' called Sophie.

Standing up on their stirrups, they all grinned,

poised like jockeys going around a racetrack.

Crystal was strong beneath Poppy. It was the most exhilarating feeling, being in control of such a big animal, feeling as one as they rocketed along. Looking down for a second, Poppy watched Crystal's hooves pounding on the ground. She let her hands fall to rest on her pony's neck. This was the feeling she lived for, the reason she was so excited about learning to ride cross-country. She wanted to fly, soar over jumps and gallop across fields. Because when she was riding like this, she didn't think about anything else but her horse.

Poppy glanced at Milly riding beside her, and received a smile in return. Poppy beamed back and enjoyed a secret chuckle at Joe's neck, which was flattened out, as if he was trying to keep his nose ahead of the other two ponies. Poppy had a theory that Joe secretly wished he was a Thoroughbred racehorse. Joe always wanted to be first, jumped higher than the rest and was generally a mischief-maker. Just like his rider, thought Poppy with a smirk.

Poppy looked over at Katie, who was riding on her other side. She seemed completely at ease in the saddle. She was still seated, leaning forward, her hands steady above Cody's neck. Despite being head over heels in love with Crystal, Poppy had to admit that Cody was the most handsome of the three ponies. His golden coat gleamed in the sunlight, and his white tail flowed out behind him. Even the excited canter he was doing now was balanced and graceful, as if he could be in the show jumping ring rather than racing across a field, flanked by his stable mates. A true Barbie horse, Poppy thought.

Aunt Sophie pulled back to a trot, and Poppy reined Crystal in slightly. She noticed that Joe took longer to slow down, ending up in front of them all.

'The creek's over there,' said Sophie, pointing ahead. 'We'll just trot over so the horses aren't blowing when we stop.'

Poppy followed her aunt's lead, turning her head to watch two large kangaroos lying in the sun nearby. There were probably more close by, hiding from the sun and sight in the bush. The kangaroos wouldn't do them any harm, she knew, so long as they kept their distance. Although, Uncle Mark's story played out in her head; he had told her about a big roo that had stolen his lunch one day, and how he'd almost had a boxing match with it before deciding to walk away from both his lunch and the roo – it was twice his size, after all!

Aunt Sophie waved them on as a smaller kangaroo moved through the nearby trees and came out into a clearing. Poppy couldn't help thinking how lucky she was to be there, but then felt the worry come back again. If they were caught looking for the stolen horses on private property, where Poppy knew they weren't allowed, could this all end? She knew Crystal was still on trial for another week, so it wouldn't exactly be hard for her aunt and uncle to give the pony back. But they wouldn't do that, would they? She couldn't stand it if they did.

She knew, too, that if they were caught, then she'd be sent home as punishment. That was not something she wanted. Not yet. Not while Tom was safely away from it all with his friend on holiday. Because Poppy needed to be away, too. She needed a break from having to cook and clean and look after her brother. She needed a break from seeing her mum like that.

CHAPTER TWELVE

Making a Splash

The air was warm, the sun was beating down, and Poppy was hot. She watched as Jupiter neared the water first, balking to start with and then taking a step in. Poppy noticed that the land around the creek was still pretty green, with grasses overhanging the creek and the low-hanging branches of the blue gum trees creating a dappled shade. She bet the kangaroos were sticking close to here because they had a good water supply; it was getting pretty dry in lots of places already, and summer had only just started. The creek was shaded and so hidden from sight, the dirt making way for sand as they neared.

'Come on, bring them in,' Aunt Sophie said.

It wasn't often Poppy had the chance just to hang out with her aunt like this. Back when she was really young, on her first few holidays to the farm, they'd ridden together almost every day. But that was before Sophie was running a riding school, training for the World Champs dressage squad and helping Mark with his new vet practice. Poppy struggled to remember the last time they'd been on horseback at the same time, and realised that it was before Milly and Katie had first arrived – more than a week ago.

Poppy urged Crystal on with her legs, but the pony would only go a few steps. Instead of walking into the water, Crystal stopped and snorted, her nostrils flaring out as she pawed the sandy ground. Milly was kicking Joe, laughing at the same time. He ended up taking a big lunging jump at the water, and Milly was shrieking the whole time.

'Encourage them,' called Sophie. 'Make it fun!'

'Come on, Crystal, go, go, go,' chanted Poppy. Her pony was nervous, she could feel it, and it was her job to give her confidence. 'Come on, you can do it,' she said, this time in a quieter voice.

Crystal's snorting became louder, but she lifted one front leg gingerly.

'Good girl!'

The forward leg movement turned into a pawing motion, and Crystal started to splash at the water, sending it everywhere.

'Crystal!' Poppy squealed, pushing harder with her legs. 'No splashing, get in!'

Crystal did move forward, all fear suddenly gone, but it had fast turned into a game. Crystal alternated with each foot, pawing and splashing. Poppy's face was sprinkled with droplets, her arms were wet, and her jodhpurs were soaking.

Katie had coaxed Cody in eventually, and now stood next to a patient Jupiter, who was regarding the ponies as if he was the old grandfather – happy to watch but certainly not impressed about getting wet.

'Arrgghhh!'

The loud scream made Poppy jump. Even the birds in the trees took flight, cockatoos squawking as they beat their wings and left the creek in a big mob. Poppy saw her aunt spring from the saddle and land knee-deep in the water. Milly had taken a tumble into the water because Joe had dropped at the knees. He was submerged in the creek, saddle and all, with the naughtiest look on his face that Poppy had ever seen.

'Milly!' Sophie waded over to a disorientated Milly, hefting her up from the water and supporting her. 'Are you okay?'

'What happened?' asked Poppy.

Milly looked around, her cheeks burning a bright red. It was the first time Poppy had ever seen her look so embarrassed about anything. Milly coughed up water and sneezed loudly.

'I, ah, don't know.' She looked confused. 'All I know is that one minute I was sitting up on Joe, laughing, and the next he just dropped. I thought he was having a heart attack or something!'

Aunt Sophie gave her a tug toward the bank, keeping an arm around her. 'The little rascal,' she laughed. 'I haven't seen a horse do that in years.'

Remaining in Crystal's saddle, Poppy grappled for Joe's reins and led the dripping horse from the water, making him follow her. She passed the reins back to her friend, who still looked stunned.

'I can't believe he did that!' Milly squeaked.

'It's going to be a wet ride home, that's for sure,' said Aunt Sophie, looking down at her own soaked-through jodhpurs and giggling at Milly. 'But worth it, right?'

Poppy laughed. 'Right.'

Katie was smiling, and even Milly seemed to have forgotten that she was annoyed at being teased.

'You girls are lucky that I remember what it was like to be horse mad and desperate to spend every day in the saddle,' Aunt Sophie told them. 'So long as you keep behaving so well, this is going to work out perfectly. I'm so excited to have the three of you here.'

Poppy gulped. Ugh. It made her worry all over again about what they had planned for tomorrow.

'We love it here! We won't let you down,' said Milly.

Poppy rolled her eyes. Enough with the butter-wouldn't-melt-in-your-mouth look, she thought, almost angry. Milly knew exactly what they could do to let her aunt down, and snooping around on Old Smithy's farm was probably top of the list.

'Oh, and I forgot to tell you all,' said Aunt Sophie as she remounted her horse. 'Entry forms are available for the Pony Club Gymkhana, so we need to work out what you want to enter. I think we'll put dressage training on hold and focus on what you girls are most interested in.'

Poppy couldn't help herself, she let out a whoop of excitement, and the others did exactly the same.

'I hope that wasn't a cheer for the lack of dressage training?' Sophie said with a scowl before laughing.

They all shook heads in unison. Poppy for one loved the idea of dressage, but she was far more interested in jumping and games. Who wanted to be riding in an arena when you could be flying over jumps or, better still, racing around barrels and bending poles?

CHAPTER THIRTEEN

No Turning Back

'Mark will be staying down in the stables tonight so you girls can get a good sleep,' Sophie said from the doorway.

Aunt Sophie's words echoed through Poppy's muddled, sleep-deprived brain as she slumped on the sofa. It wasn't even eight o'clock yet, and she was so tired that her eyes were burning and her head was thumping.

'Thanks,' she mumbled.

Katie just raised her head slightly as she lay on the floor with Milly, who gave a thumbs up.

'I can't have you all feeling so exhausted. Get to bed now, and you'll feel better in the morning.'

Poppy didn't need any further encouragement. She flopped her feet down, tried to shake off the pins and needles in her legs, then stood up, offering one hand to Katie. Milly grabbed it instead and hauled herself up.

'Night, Aunt Sophie,' Poppy said.

'Night, Mrs D,' the other two chanted.

Sophie smiled at them as they filed past, blowing a kiss in their general direction.

'Pop, did you call your mum tonight?' she asked.

Poppy nodded. 'Yeah, after dinner. I had to leave a message.'

'Okay. I'm sure she'll call back tomorrow then. Night, girls,' Aunt Sophie said.

They hadn't even reached the stairs before Milly started pestering.

'We're all set for tomorrow, right?'

'I guess,' Poppy murmured.

'Are you sure?' asked Katie, whispering as they plodded up the stairs. 'Mrs D was so nice today, and I don't want to disappoint her.'

Milly was having none of it. 'We owe those horses,' she said, barring the bedroom door so they couldn't get past her.

'Come on, just let us get to bed,' moaned Katie.

'Not before you say yes,' Milly insisted.

Poppy put her head down and charged into Milly's arms. 'Milly, come on, let us through!'

'Not until you say yes!' Milly insisted.

'Okay, I'll do it,' Poppy said. 'Who ever thought saving horses would be such hard work!'

Poppy knew she was being grumpy. She was tired, and realised that she was probably worried about her mum, too. It always worried her when her mum didn't answer and she had to leave a voicemail. She also just wasn't sure about going through with their plan, even if she had thought it was what she wanted to do. She had so much to lose if it went wrong. But then, how could she give up on horses that might need her help?

As her head hit the pillow, she felt her body relax into the comfy mattress and soft sheets. Not even her worrying could stop her from sleeping tonight.

The day was already warm, and Poppy squinted up at the sky. White clouds drifted over, and the wind blew lightly on her arms. It was exactly the kind of day she loved, perfect for a trail ride, but she had butterflies twirling in her stomach as those worrying thoughts from last night whirred round her head. She took comfort in the familiar laughter of a kookaburra, probably the same one she'd hated the morning before for waking her.

'You ready?' Milly gave her a nudge on the shoulder.

No, she thought. I'm not really ready for sneaking onto forbidden land and getting into a heap of trouble if we're caught.

'Yeah, I guess,' she lied.

Katie appeared then, leading an immaculately turned-out Cody. His golden coat was gleaming, and she had put his white saddle blanket and matching tendon boots on. Poppy glanced over at her pony, tacked up and ready to go. Crystal's grey coat was flecked with freckles, and although she might not be as beautiful in colour as the palomino, she was gorgeous in Poppy's eyes. Her head was alert and pretty, her big brown eyes expressive as she stared back at Poppy. Her body was perfectly proportioned, with fine and elegant legs.

Poppy tried not to think about what could

happen if they were caught. Would her aunt be tempted to take her new pony away from her as punishment? Or, just as bad, send her home? She shuddered at the thought. But, after a good night's sleep, she had to agree with Milly, and felt sure that they were doing the right thing. What if the horses were in that barn all along and no one ever found them? Poppy knew that if any one of their ponies had been stolen, they'd want it to be rescued, no matter what. And if trespassing was what it took, then so be it.

Joe stamped impatiently at the ground, and, not for the first time, Poppy marvelled at how similar Milly was to her pony. Crystal on the other hand looked on eagerly, head cocked in her rider's direction, just like Cody.

Poppy unbuckled her pink halter and tightened the girth, putting her stirrups up two holes as well. They had put them down one for dressage practice the day before, but she wanted them at a comfortable length for trail riding and jumping. There would be nothing worse than having them too long and losing a stirrup iron when they jumped the gate. Goose pimples tickled her back and arms, but she did her best to ignore them. They were saving horses, she reminded herself. It was all worth it.

'Come on!' Milly was looking down at her, already mounted.

'I'm coming, I'm coming,' Poppy muttered back.

Katie swung into the saddle about the same time, and they gave each other a quick glance. Poppy was certain that Katie would pull out if she did, but she wasn't about to go back on her word. Not now. They were all in this together, and there was only one thing to do: be brave and not look back.

The horses jumped and jittered on the ride, but Poppy couldn't blame them. She knew herself that she was as nervous as could be, and she bet Milly and Katie were, too. A horse could always sense its rider's mood, and she'd read somewhere that it only took minutes for the animal to match its rider's heartbeat. So if her heart was racing, Crystal's was, too.

Crystal started to jig-jog again.

'How about a trot?' Poppy suggested to the others.

Poppy pushed her pony on, but she hardly even had to squeeze. Crystal broke into a bouncy trot, leaving Poppy fighting with her head to slow her down. She remembered all the instruction Sophie had given her, and sat a little deeper. It isn't about using your hands, it's about slowing the horse with your seat. She sat deep, hands steady, rising slowly, and Crystal responded. Joe danced close behind them, though, and she was sure Cody would be breathing down their necks soon, too.

'What's the plan?' she called over her shoulder to Milly.

'Get in and out as quick as we can,' Milly yelled back.

'Anyone thought about how we are actually going to get into the barn?' came the logical voice of Katie.

'What d'ya mean?' Milly clearly wasn't impressed.

'I mean it could be locked, dummy,' Katie said.

Poppy hadn't thought about that. How would they get in if it was locked?

The horses had calmed down a little now, still excited but not quite so jumpy. Poppy dropped her hands a little lower and rubbed at Crystal's mane. She had been so busy since the others had arrived, thinking about their plan to save the stolen horses, keeping up with her chores and riding, that she had hardly taken time to just enjoy hanging out with Crystal. To enjoy the fact that she had her own pony.

She'd do anything to be like before. So long as she could still have Crystal, of course. But before, when she used to come to the farm and have nothing but horses on her mind, because she'd had nothing else to think about. She'd been a kid who did kid stuff with no worries.

While she was here, she just wanted to be 'Poppy the rider'. 'Poppy with her own pony'. Not 'Poppy, the kid without a dad, and a mum who'd forgotten how to look after her'.

The old rickety gate that marked the boundary appeared ahead, half-hidden, partly obscured by overgrown blackberry brambles. It pulled her from her thoughts and she brought Crystal back to a walk, calling out whoa as she did so. The others did the same, stopping on a clearing of grass.

'This is it then,' said Poppy. Her voice wavered

slightly but she kept her chin up.

'Well, what are we waiting for?' Milly's voice was strong and brave. The exact opposite of how Poppy felt.

'So just to check,' said Katie, receiving a roll of the eyes from Milly, 'we're going to race to the barn, somehow manage to get in, and then take a look around, right?'

Milly nodded. Poppy slowly exhaled, trying to stay calm.

'And what if we do actually find them in there?' she continued.

'Duh. We race back and tell Mrs D.'

'Duh,' said Poppy straight back at Milly. 'Then we have to explain how we found them in the first place.'

'We could always just call the police anonymously,' suggested Katie. 'I have my mobile.'

'Yeah, whatever,' said Milly. 'We can work out the details on the way back, once we've found them.'

'And if he shows up?' asked Poppy.

'We couldn't be that unlucky for him to see us on his land twice,' said Milly.

'I've taken care of it,' interrupted Katie.

What? How could Katie have taken care of it?

'How?'

'Just don't worry. If he captures us, the Delaneys will know where to find us. Eventually.'

Poppy hoped for their sake that Katie was right.

'Oh no!'

Poppy turned to look at Katie, startled by the worried look on her friend's face.

'What?'

'We don't have any signal here. If we do get in any trouble, we won't be able to call for help.'

Milly sighed dramatically. 'Forget about all the things that could go wrong and just think about why we're doing this. Come on!'

Poppy gulped and looked ahead, not wanting to look at Katie again in case she lost her nerve. Milly was right. They were here to save the horses. They just had to make sure they didn't get caught.

CHAPTER FOURTEEN

Trouble

Poppy had that strange feeling of déjà vu. Like she'd been here, done this before. Only, unlike last time, she was a lot more alert to what was happening around them. The ponies thundered over the old gate, ears pricked and enjoying the 'game'. She held Crystal in check, keeping her canter steady, and let her eyes rove back and forward, surveying the land. She would probably *smell* his truck coming this time, her senses were so alert!

Up ahead, Milly threw her arm out and waved them forward. The big barn was getting closer by the second, and Poppy's heart was thumping so hard in her chest, she thought it might actually jump out.

They all reined back to a trot, following Milly's lead as they arrived at the barn. Milly waited until they had caught up to her and were riding three abreast before she spoke in a low voice.

'The door must be around the other side.'

Poppy tried to catch her breath but her mouth felt too dry, like she'd swallowed a bucket of sand.

'Should one of us stay around this side and keep look out?' she suggested, finally finding her tongue.

Katie nodded ferociously, her head moving up and down. 'Yes.'

'No!' said Milly at the same time. 'We need to stick together.'

Poppy looked from one friend to the other. Before she could speak, a loud thud caught all of their attention.

'What was that?' she gasped, forgetting the whisper rule.

Two pairs of scared eyes looked back at her. She knew they were wondering the same thing.

'That sounded suspiciously like a horse kicking,' hissed Milly. 'I told you I heard something the other day!'

Poppy gulped. She'd heard it the other day, too,

only this time it was louder.

Thump! There it was again.

'We've got to get in there!' shouted Milly.

This was it, thought Poppy. Their one chance to save the stolen horses.

'We can't ride our horses in,' said Poppy. 'One of us will need to hold them while the other two go in.'

'Uh-uh, we all go in.' Milly was firm.

Katie rode Cody over to a sparse row of trees and started to inspect the branches.

'I reckon we can tether them here,' she called.

'Sshhhh!' hissed Milly and Poppy.

Katie gave a shrug and dismounted, then pulled Cody's reins over his head and wound them around a branch. He didn't look like he was going anywhere.

Poppy followed Katie's lead, walking Crystal over to tie her next to Cody.

Milly did the same. 'This is it, girls,' she said. 'Let's find those stolen horses.'

The barn was huge, much larger looking than when they'd been on horseback. Poppy turned her back to the barn, eyes peeled for any sign of danger.

'I need a hand,' said Milly.

Poppy reluctantly turned back round. The big wooden bar had to be pushed along to allow them access, and they all heaved as hard as they could to open it, the hinges creaking. Another loud thump echoed out, louder this time. It just had to be a horse kicking out for help!

With one quick glance over her shoulder, Poppy and her friends entered the barn. The door shut with a bang behind them, and Poppy's heart dropped through the floor of her stomach as soon as her eyes adjusted to the dim light. She clung tightly on to Katie's arm.

'What the...' Her voice trailed off. She had no idea what to say.

'I think we'd better get out of here,' said Katie.

Poppy still couldn't believe her eyes. There, in front of them, were cattle. A bang, louder than any they had heard from outside, vibrated through the huge barn. Then another. Poppy scanned the interior, sure that she'd see a horse somewhere, but then her eyes locked on what was making all that noise.

A big, huge, ginormous bull was kicking the wall

of the barn as hard as he could, and was now looking in their direction. He looked angry. Mean, even.

'We need to get out of here now,' whispered Poppy, squeezing Katie harder.

All the cows were huge, but this big beast was on another level. Poppy had been on enough farm rounds with her uncle to know the difference between a cow and a bull, and that, most definitely, was a bull. She was just pleased all the animals were behind high dividers, so the bull couldn't hurt them.

'What are these cattle doing in here?' asked Milly. 'Don't people usually keep cattle in paddocks rather than hidden away in dark barns?'

'Let's just go,' Poppy said.

But when another loud thump resonated through the barn, one glance at the now-still bull sent a shiver up and down Poppy's spine. It was a bang that sounded nothing like the others had.

'Katie...' Poppy's voice was cut off by a thundering voice.

'What the heck are you girls doing in here?'

They all turned to find a man in the entrance to the barn. He'd opened it up fully, and the big door was swinging from its hinges.

It was Old Smithy, and the light behind him was making him look scarier than ever before. His hair stood on end. He looked even angrier than the bull. He was old, but he was tall and wide. He looked strong, stronger than them.

The cattle moved behind the girls, but Poppy didn't dare turn around. The animals were secure. They couldn't hurt them. But this guy? She shuddered, scared of him. They hadn't even found the stolen horses!

'I asked you what you're doing here!' his voice echoed around the barn, making them all jump.

'Run!' screamed Milly, making a lunge for the open space between Old Smithy and the door. 'Run for your lives!'

Poppy didn't need any further encouragement. She sprung from her toes and made for the door. She could feel Katie right behind her. Katie darted out to the left, following Milly, and Poppy went right. But the old guy was fast. He lunged first for Milly, grabbing her by the arm, and then he made a grab for Katie. Their screams echoed in the big barn, Milly's the loudest of all.

'No!' yelled Poppy, grabbing hold of Katie and

fighting to keep hold of her

Katie held on to Poppy, as if worried he would grab her, too. But Milly took them all by surprise. She bit down hard on Old Smithy's arm. He yelled and let her go, looking shocked. It was just a second before he pulled himself together again, but it was all they needed.

The girls ran as fast as they could, back to where they had left the ponies tethered. But the ponies weren't there.

'Oh no!' Poppy yelled, running ahead of the others, panic surging through her as she scanned the land, searching for Crystal. 'Where are they?'

Milly was running next to her, and Poppy could hear Katie behind her crying, sobbing between breaths as she ran, but Poppy didn't slow down.

The rumble of an engine signalled that Old Smithy was in his truck. They'd never be able to outrun him now.

'Quick! Over here!' Poppy cried to the others as she dove into the bushes, prickly branches tearing at her face. Katie and Milly jumped in behind her. It was a huge area of shrubs, nestled around the base of a small wood of large pine trees, but Poppy was under no illusion that they were safe. He knew where they were heading, and he'd find them. Eventually.

'What are we going to do?' cried Katie.

'Didn't you say you had it covered?' asked Milly.

Poppy looked at Katie, hoping her friend really did have them covered.

'I left a note on Cody's stable for the Delaneys. I thought they would find it when they came back in, if we weren't home. But I'd also planned on having a phone that worked!'

'It could be hours before they see it!' said Milly.

Poppy closed her eyes and tried to calm herself. Her heart was beating fast with nerves. 'We need to find one of the ponies,' she said. Her voice was shaky, but so was her entire body. She was shaking in fear. 'Then one of us can get back for help.' She wanted so desperately to find the stolen horses, but right now they needed to alert her aunt or uncle that they were in serious trouble.

Poppy scanned the surrounding fields. Cows to the left, cows to the right. Weird that the cattle out here weren't like the ones in the barn, she thought. The cows in the barn were light brown. These are black and white. And there are no ponies – theirs or stolen ones. Poppy ran her eyes back over the land again.

'Oh my gosh!' Poppy's hand flew up to cover her mouth.

'What?' Milly's eyes popped wide. Katie looked like she was going to start crying again.

'The cows,' said Poppy. 'Look over there.'

Katie and Milly's eyes followed Poppy's point.

'He hid the coloured horses in with the dairy cows!' Poppy was almost annoyed with herself. She had spotted the cows two days ago, but she'd never even thought to make the connection, and the others clearly hadn't, either. But there they were, clear as day. Black-and-white horses camouflaged among a hundred or so black-and-white cows in the paddock. They'd been right about Old Smithy all along!

Poppy heard gravel crunch nearby, and pulled her friends back into the bushes. Old Smithy was getting close. Poppy spied his ute parked next to a tree, the engine still rumbling. She could feel the hairs prickle on the back of her neck.

'So he does have them!' whispered Milly excitedly.

Even Katie looked happier. 'At least this wasn't all for nothing. Even if he does capture us.'

'We've got to get back to Starlight,' said Poppy. She was excited about what they had discovered, but it didn't change the fact that they needed help. It wouldn't be long before Old Smithy found their hiding place – she could hear his heavy breathing just beyond the bushes.

Milly ignored her. 'I can only count four,' she whispered. 'Do you think they're all here?'

Poppy left it to Milly and Katie to scan the paddocks while she kept an eye on Old Smithy. He'd moved away from their hiding place, and Poppy let her eyes travel from the barn they had fled to the nearby trees, searching for their lost ponies. A movement caught her eye. It was Joe. Poppy stayed still and tugged on Katie's sleeve.

'There's Joe,' she whispered.

'Can you see Crystal yet?' Katie asked.

Poppy kept watch. Cody came walking out of the trees then, which made Joe trot off, head held high. Poppy held her breath as she saw Cody's reins dangling precariously near his hooves. Then Crystal came wandering from the same direction as Cody, and Poppy almost let out a whoop of excitement.

'I'm going to make a run for it,' said Poppy, turning back to her friends. She could hardly feel her legs from squatting low, but she had to get to Crystal. She realised she'd lost track of Old Smithy. He could be anywhere. He could even have gone back to his house to get his gun. Wherever he was, Poppy knew that it was now or never, while Crystal was so close.

'Are you sure?' asked Katie.

'Why don't we all go?' suggested Milly.

Poppy stretched up to look past the bushes, then turned and shook her head.

'No. We'll never make it if we all run. He'd definitely see us and we might not be able to catch all three ponies. I'll go, jump on whichever one stays still or is close enough.' Poppy reached her hands out to touch her friends. She knew that if she had to wait for her friends to mount, it would only slow them down, and if one of them took off while another was still trying to get into the saddle with only one foot in the stirrup, it could end in a nasty accident. 'I'll race straight back to the farm and get help. Just stay hidden, okay?'

Milly and Katie squeezed her hand back, and Poppy counted to ten in her mind. She stretched one leg, ready to run, pushed her head out from the bush, took one look around to check Old Smithy wasn't there, and then sprinted.

Her feet raced along the hard-packed dirt below. She had never moved so fast in her life, and especially not in riding boots. Poppy heard a rustling noise behind her, but she didn't turn. A scream rang out loud in the air, but she didn't even slow. All Poppy wanted to do was spin around and help her friends, but she knew if she stopped, even hesitated, she might not make it back to safety. And then who would save them?

Poppy felt like she was running for her life. Her head was down and her arms were pumping against her sides, pushing her forward. Her friends continued to yell out, but Poppy only had one thing in mind. She had to make it to Crystal. She could see her pony ahead of her, grazing contentedly, and she kept on running. She caught sight of Smithy's blue ute, blurred, to the side of her vision. But Poppy's eyes stayed focused, fixed on her pony.

She willed Crystal to put her head up, to read

her mind and get ready to bolt. But the pony didn't. Poppy kept running. Her heart was pounding, and she was struggling to catch her breath. Her lungs and throat were burning, but she didn't care. All she cared about was getting to Crystal, racing home and finding help. They might be in a power-load of trouble, but right now she had to save her friends. That was all that mattered.

It seemed to take forever, but when Poppy finally reached her pony and thudded to a stop beside her, Crystal startled. But Poppy didn't have time to be gentle. She yanked Crystal's head up and untied her reins, throwing them back over her pony's head. Poppy glanced over her shoulder. She couldn't see Old Smithy, and she relaxed just a smidge. She remembered to tighten her girth, pulled her stirrups down and virtually vaulted into the saddle.

'Sorry, Crystal!' she cried as, for the first time ever, she dug her heels hard into her pony. Crystal snorted and raised her head high, acting distressed, but made for the boundary as Poppy steered her towards Starlight Stables and safety. The gate was edging closer and closer, and Poppy urged her pony to go faster. They were galloping now, thundering across the paddock. With the sound of Crystal's hooves pounding in her ears, Poppy allowed herself a quick look over her shoulder. Thankfully the other two ponies hadn't followed from where she'd left them grazing on the long grass.

She turned back, focused on what was ahead. The jump was maybe ten strides out now. Poppy pulled on the reins and sat deep, slowing Crystal back to a canter. But Crystal was really wound up now, excited by the urgency in her rider's commands, and she fought for her head, tugging back and keeping her head high. They took off too early, her jump huge – high and long – but Poppy trusted Crystal. Still, she realised she was holding her breath until she was sure that they'd cleared it. They landed heavily on the other side, and Poppy directed Crystal straight into the forest. She chanced another glance over her shoulder, but still couldn't see any sign of Old Smithy, and that almost worried her more than seeing him. She knew he had Katie and Milly. Would she be able to get help in time?

Crystal responded when Poppy squeezed her legs, and they cantered along the sandy track fast.

Branches tore at her arms, but Poppy was blinded by terror that Old Smithy would somehow catch her even though she was riding fast. A fallen log appeared in front of them but they flew over it, going faster still, Crystal not missing a beat. Poppy didn't ever remember going this fast before, but she didn't dare slow. Every second counted, and they kept going. She needed to make sure her friends were okay!

Finally, the trees began to thin, and she knew they were almost at Starlight. She started to worry that Aunt Sophie wouldn't be back yet. She had to get help, and fast! The stables were a blur in the distance ahead, and she raced towards them.

CHAPTER FIFTEEN

Help!

'Sophie!' Poppy screamed at the top of her lungs, terror resounding in her voice. 'Aunt Sophie!'

Crystal quivered beneath her, one ear flickering back to listen to the terrified screams of her rider.

'Aunt Sophie, where are you?' Her shouts were coming out as sobs now.

Footsteps thudded from the stables, and Uncle Mark came running towards her, his face creased with concern. Then Poppy saw Jupiter come flying around the corner, with Sophie kicking his sides. She had *never* seen her aunt ride him like that before.

'Poppy, what's happened?' Uncle Mark got to her first, pulling her down from Crystal's back, his arms wrapped protectively around her. 'Where are the others?'

She could hardly stop the tears that were falling down her cheeks in big plops.

'Poppy, say something!' Mark's voice sounded full of panic as he knelt down before her and put his hands on either side of her face, gently but firmly making her look at him.

'They're, they're...'

'Poppy!' Her aunt jumped from her horse and rushed over to her. 'I heard you galloping out of the forest. What's happened, honey? Has there been an accident? Where are the others?'

She looked up at her aunt, and then turned again to Mark, wishing she had never gone through with the stupid plan. The words came out in a rush, and she knew she sounded hysterical.

'Old Smithy, he caught them. They're on his property. Cody and Joe are there, too, but I managed to get away.'

'Smithy's? What on earth?' Aunt Sophie's raised eyebrows halted Poppy's tears. Poppy wanted to tell her how sorry she was. Her aunt was going to hate her, probably even send her home, but apologies could wait. Right now, she had to catch her breath and get back there. If it meant her holiday was over and she had to be sent home, then she'd take the punishment. She didn't care, as long as she saved her friends.

'We went looking for the stolen horses,' she admitted, hanging her head in shame at going behind their backs.

Uncle Mark sighed, expelling a big lungful of air. He looked angry. She'd never seen him angry before.

'You did what?' asked Aunt Sophie. Her words were clipped and her voice was low, almost a whisper. Poppy felt her aunt's disappointment with each word.

'We thought that the stolen horses were in his barn, so we went exploring, and now he's got Milly and Katie. We have to save them!'

Her uncle shook his head, and Aunt Sophie just turned her back, grabbing Crystal's reins as she did so and leading her quickly, with Jupiter, back toward the stables.

'Aren't we going to save them,' Poppy gulped, watching her aunt walk off.

'Of course we're going to save them, Poppy. Get in the truck,' said Uncle Mark as he took long strides across the gravel to where his truck was parked outside the barn.

Poppy ran to keep up. Her legs felt like jelly as she pulled herself up into the truck's back seat.

Uncle Mark slammed the door as he stepped in to the driver's side. 'You knew not to go over there, Poppy,' he said without looking at her. 'Why would you disobey me? Especially after what we told you the other night?'

'I know, but...' Poppy started to tell Mark that they'd found the missing horses, but her aunt appeared from the stables, shouting to them as she ran towards the truck.

'I've called the police,' called Aunt Sophie. 'They're on their way over there, too.'

'Come on, let's go get your friends,' said her uncle. Sophie slid into the passenger seat next to him, then he put his foot down hard on the accelerator. The wheels spun in response against the gravel on the driveway, and the car lurched forward, speeding down the driveway.

Trees and bushes whirred past the window, and

Poppy pressed her nose against the glass, welcoming its coldness against her hot face. She was terrified. She could hardly breathe.

'Poppy, I do have to point out that you girls trespassed onto Smithy's land, and he is the one neighbour, and you know this, who does not allow us over there. He does not like his stock disrupted, and, quite frankly, he's not the sort of person we want you around,' said Uncle Mark.

'But...'

'No buts, Poppy. You know exactly why we didn't want you going over there.'

'But we found the horses!' Poppy cried. She swallowed and sucked in a big breath.

'You what?' Her aunt spun around in her seat, and Poppy saw Uncle Mark's eyes watching her in the rear-view mirror.

'That's what I was trying to tell you!' said Poppy, nearly jumping off the seat she was so worried about her friends. 'We got it wrong. We thought that they were in the barn, but he had them disguised in the paddocks with the black-and-white dairy cows.'

The car went silent. Poppy didn't know what else to say.

'You're still in trouble, Poppy,' said her aunt.

Poppy gulped. 'I know.'

'I think you need to ring the police again,' said Uncle Mark in a low voice. 'Make sure they're definitely on their way. Now.'

If something had happened to Milly and Katie... Poppy didn't want to finish that sentence. But suddenly, all she could think about was what it might look like to see a man get his jaw broken in a fight, like her aunt had described to them at the dinner table the other night.

In no time at all, they'd arrived at Old Smithy's place. Poppy knew her uncle had been speeding, and she worried about her friends even more, because Mark never usually went fast in areas where kangaroos or other wildlife could be crossing.

Uncle Mark and Aunt Sophie jumped out of the car, and Poppy obeyed their orders. She was not to move a muscle. She didn't know if she could even if she tried. Her fear for her friends had her glued to the spot.

She watched her aunt and uncle run to the farmhouse. She spotted a police car already parked outside the house, and that comforted her.

It seemed like forever that she was waiting for someone to appear, thrumming her fingers against her thighs. She had gone over the dressage alphabet in her mind, practising where and when she would have to turn for her first dressage test at pony club, but it was no good. She couldn't concentrate. Besides, she might not even make it to actual Pony Club, let alone the big gymkhana. Not after all this.

A flicker of movement from the corner of her eye made her sit up straight in the seat. She could see them all walking from the house. A policeman was following behind Milly and Katie, talking to her aunt and uncle. There was no sign of Smithy.

Still Poppy didn't move, though. They came closer to the truck, and Poppy could see that Milly and Katie looked terrified, and that they'd been crying, their eyes all red and puffy. She watched, holding her breath, expecting them to be put in the police car, but they kept walking towards her while her aunt and uncle stood talking to the policeman.

Poppy pushed the door open to let them in, and her eyes locked on Katie's.

'What happened?' Her voice was hardly more than a whisper.

Katie just flopped into the back seat and huddled up next to Poppy. Milly jumped in after her, and slammed the door.

'What a disaster,' said Milly.

'Did he hurt you?'

Katie just shook her head, and so Poppy looked to Milly for a reply.

'He found us in the bushes and marched us back to his house. I thought he was going to break my arm, he was holding it so tight. Then he called the police and hardly said a thing to us.'

Poppy squeezed both of their hands, tight.

'Except to tell us that we were in big trouble,' added Katie. 'He said that we'd regret ever stepping foot on his land, and told us not to move.'

'Yeah, there was that,' agreed Milly. 'Then the police showed up, told us that trespassing and breaking into someone's property was a big deal.'

'Didn't you tell them that he had stolen the horses?' asked Poppy. 'Why did *he* call the police?'

'I know!' exclaimed Milly. 'That's what *I* wondered. But then the Ds arrived, and Sophie told us to go wait in the car. I guess he had no idea we'd figured him out and seen the horses in the paddock.'

They all looked at one another, and Poppy found herself in a group hug as Katie threw one arm around each of her friends.

'We're all safe now, though,' Katie said. 'Thanks for riding to our rescue, Poppy.'

Poppy smiled back, but noticed another policeman emerged from the house.

'Uh-oh,' said Poppy as the smile dropped from her face.

'We're still going to be in big trouble, aren't we?' said Katie, although Poppy knew that she wasn't really asking. They all knew.

'Do you think they'll take our horses away and send us home?' asked Milly.

Poppy met their gaze, but looked down. The thing was, she had no idea what they would do. She had never been in trouble with her aunt and uncle before. There was a lot at stake. They might have saved the missing horses, but they had still lied about what they were up to. Would Sophie and Mark ever forgive her? Poppy would rather be sent home than see her friends lose their ponies. She didn't know how to tell them that all their ponies were still on trial. Would her aunt and uncle send the ponies back?

As they sat in the back of the truck, misery painted across their faces, Poppy wondered about how quickly they'd all become friends. It seemed like she'd known Milly and Katie her entire lifetime already. She wasn't ready to say goodbye to them.

And then there was the thought of going home. What if Sophie and Mark did send her back? Poppy closed her eyes and let her head fall back against the headrest. Going home was something she really did not want to face, not yet.

Poppy looked across at Aunt Sophie, who was riding Cody along the track next to her. Sophie dwarfed the palamino as she rode him, with her long legs touching down to his knees. Poppy was riding Joe, and it had been over ten minutes now since they'd left Old Smithy's, and still her aunt hadn't spoken to her. They weren't even halfway home yet. For once, Poppy almost wished she wasn't in the saddle, but there had been no other way to get the ponies home, so she'd volunteered to ride with Sophie. She wasn't even able to enjoy the fact she was riding such a fun pony, who somehow hadn't picked up on the mood around him and was dancing along, wanting to trot.

Poppy couldn't take it any more. 'Aunt Sophie, I'm so sorry we let you down,' she said, breaking the silence. She kept her head low, her mind churning over all the things she could say to stop her aunt from sending her home. She realised she was going to have to tell her the truth about her mum.

'I know,' said Aunt Sophie, but she wouldn't look at Poppy.

Then there was silence again. Poppy hated it.

'I just, well, I want you to know that I didn't want to do it behind your back, but we were just certain he had the horses in there. At least we saved them, right?'

Sophie dodged the fallen log by going around it, and Poppy followed her lead. She would have loved to see what it was like to jump Joe, but she didn't dare leave Sophie's side.

'I can accept you made a mistake, Poppy, and I can probably understand why you did it, but you've put me in a very awkward position. Not to mention disappointed me. I have no other choice but to inform your mum, and the other girls' parents, too. I trusted you, and you've broken that trust.'

Poppy's eyes welled up with tears. This was it. She was going to lose her first and only pony, her holiday here was over for good, and she was going to lose her two new friends.

'I have to go home?' She hoped with all her heart that it wasn't true. Poppy watched Sophie rein Cody in before giving her a long hard look.

'Poppy, I'm not going to send you home. Don't be ridiculous.'

Poppy couldn't believe her ears. The tears stopped pretty quick, and her heart began to thump. She was still scared, though. Worried about what her mum would do when she found out. She felt her eyes well up again.

'But, you're going to tell my mum?' she whispered.

'Yes.' Aunt Sophie didn't hesitate. 'You've left me with no other option.'

Poppy nodded, but it didn't stop the tears from streaming down her cheeks. She didn't want to cry in front of her aunt, but she couldn't help it.

'Poppy?' Aunt Sophie asked. 'Poppy, it's okay. I'm sure she…'

'You can't,' Poppy blurted.

Sophie made Cody halt, so Poppy did the same. 'Look at me, Poppy. What's really going on here?'

Poppy bit down on her lip, but it was still quivering.

'You've really let me down, but it doesn't mean I don't want you here, Pop, if that's what you're worried about?'

She shook her head. She had to tell her aunt. 'I don't want you to tell my mum because she isn't, um,' Poppy didn't know how to say it.

Aunt Sophie dropped the reins and put her hands on her thighs. 'Are things not going so well at home? I know it must be so hard since your dad passed, but when I spoke to your mum last week, she said everything was going okay.'

Poppy leaned forward and slung her arms around Joe's neck, stroking him, needing to touch him. 'Mum hasn't been okay for ages,' she admitted. 'Not since Dad died.'

Aunt Sophie frowned. She looked upset.

'Tell me, Poppy. Tell me what's happening. She's my sister, and that means it's okay to confide in me. I can help. You're not betraying her by being honest.'

Poppy sighed, and the words rushed out of her.

'She doesn't get out of bed until we're home from school sometimes, and I have to keep pretending with everyone that things are normal. But they're not.' Poppy looked up and tried to smile at her aunt, but she wasn't able to stop talking now she'd started. 'I try to get her to eat, and to keep the house tidy in case someone comes around. Because I know she'll be fine soon. It's just that she misses Dad so much. And I have to look after Tom.'

Poppy kept Joe still as Aunt Sophie nudged Cody closer to her, and reached out to touch Poppy's leg. Sophie's hand felt warm and strong, even through Poppy's jodhpurs.

'I wish you'd told me sooner, Poppy. You could have phoned me and asked for help. I'm always, always here for you, no matter what.'

Poppy couldn't help it, the tears just kept coming. 'But I don't want Mum to get into trouble,' she managed to say between sobs.

'She won't, honey, she won't. I'll make sure of it. You need to trust me.'

She did trust her aunt Sophie, more than anyone else. She was the one person in the world who probably could help.

'I'm not saying that what you did here today was excusable, but I am pleased the horses were found, and I'm glad you finally trusted me enough to tell me what's going on at home.'

Poppy waited for the 'but'. She knew it was coming. Poppy hoped she'd done the right thing in telling her aunt.

'Don't worry about your mum, Pop. I want you to be a kid while you're here, and let me be the adult, okay? You're still in trouble, but I don't want you to have any responsibilities other than your pony while you're staying with us.' She sighed. 'I'll get on the phone as soon as we're back and organise some help for your mum, and I'll take you back to Melbourne myself when it's time. We'll go together, and I can talk to her then about you staying longer. Your brother can come here, too, if he can't stay longer with his friend.'

Poppy didn't say a word because she didn't know what to say. She wanted to say 'thank you', but that didn't even touch on everything that she was feeling. Relief, hope…

Any punishment, slavery even, so long as she could stay at the farm and her mum didn't find out.

She didn't want to cause her any more worry.

She only hoped the other girls wouldn't be sent home either.

CHAPTER SIXTEEN

Punishment

Poppy tried not to wriggle in her spot between Milly and Katie on the sofa. Uncle Mark looked very uncomfortable, facing them on the chair. Aunt Sophie, on the other hand, was walking back and forward in front of them.

'I know you girls were doing your best to help, but doing things behind our backs is unacceptable,' said Aunt Sophie.

'But Mrs D...' Milly interrupted.

Sophie raised her hand and pointed to her lips. 'Quiet.'

Poppy gulped. She had never seen her aunt angry, and she had *never* heard her speak like that.

'According to the police, the horses you found were the ones reported stolen. Smithy had more disguised in another field with other cattle, and he has been arrested.' She paused and smiled at them. Poppy had never been so relieved to see her aunt smile before. 'You'll also be pleased to know that you have solved another mystery,' Sophie told them.

Poppy looked at Milly and Katie. They looked as surprised as she was.

'Apparently, the bull in with those cows in the barn was also stolen. He was worth a small fortune, and he'd been taken from out of town. That man was a horse and cattle rustler.'

Poppy couldn't believe it. Their hunch that there was something fishy about the barn had been true!

'Anyway, I've made my mind up, and Mark agrees, about what your punishment will be.'

All three girls looked at Mark, who was clearly embarrassed about having to dish out punishment. Poppy was sure her aunt had decided how to reprimand them and was making Uncle Mark tell them.

'Please, please don't tell my parents,' pleaded Katie. Poppy felt for her friend, who looked so distressed.

'I have a right mind to send you all home,' said Aunt Sophie, sitting on the arm of the chair next to Uncle Mark.

Poppy felt her eyes widen and drew in a sharp breath. She hoped Aunt Sophie hadn't really changed her mind about sending her home.

'But we're not going to send any of you home,' Uncle Mark quickly added.

Poppy let out a deep sigh of relief.

'We have tried to understand the reasons behind what you did,' Mark continued. 'And since the police are so pleased that the horse thief has been apprehended, we see no reason to be too hard.'

Aunt Sophie nodded. 'We'd seen firsthand the temper Smithy had, and we knew he didn't care about his animals like we do, but we had no idea he was a criminal. No one out here did.'

'So while we know that it was a good thing you caught him red-handed, it was still dangerous, and you betrayed our trust,' continued Uncle Mark.

'It was very irresponsible, girls, and so we are

going to take away all your riding privileges for the next five days,' said Aunt Sophie. 'We are both prepared to give you a second chance, but make no mistake that if you do anything like this again, your ponies will be returned and your holiday here will be over.'

Poppy gulped. They were lucky her aunt and uncle were so understanding. But five days? That was almost a week! Their holiday was only four weeks long, so it sounded like forever. But still, Poppy knew she was lucky to be here, and the punishment could have been a lot worse – her holiday could have been over.

'In addition to your riding privileges being taken away, you will have to complete theory every day. I also want you to clean all the water troughs, and scrub down the walls of the stables.' Sophie looked at each of them in turn, and they all three stayed silent.

Poppy wondered what the other girls' faces looked like, but didn't dare turn away from her aunt. Aunt Sophie fixed her with a stare, which Poppy knew meant that she wanted to talk to her alone later.

'I want an apology from each of you, and a promise that you will tell me before you head off on any other adventures. If you have been good, you will be permitted to trail ride again after the five days are up. Otherwise it will be arena-only riding. Permanently.'

'Oh, we'll be good,' said Poppy, prepared to agree to anything so long as she could stay here.

'Yeah, sooo good,' agreed Milly.

Katie just nodded and smiled.

'With no riding practice, you'll all be very unprepared for the practice gymkhana, not to mention behind on learning for your first Pony Club rally, but it'll have to do.'

'Will we still make it to Pony Club though?' asked Poppy.

She'd been wanting to join the local Pony Club for ages. It would be awful to miss out when she'd looked forward to it for so long.

'Yes, you'll still make it. Pony Club day is on Sunday, after our gymkhana here.'

Aunt Sophie sighed and shook her head, but she had a faint smile playing over her lips. Poppy relaxed, smiling back at her aunt.

172

'Just don't let me down again, girls, okay? We don't need the extra worry.'

Poppy was drenched, her legs saturated from cleaning the water trough. Milly was also up to her elbows on the other side of the fence, cleaning the adjoining trough.

'It could have been a lot worse,' said Katie.

Poppy noticed that she was loitering around the edge of the muddy area, trying not to get wet and dirty. She's not going to get away with that for long with the chores Sophie had planned for us, Poppy thought.

Milly glared at Katie, her disagreement obvious. 'Like how?' she asked.

Poppy agreed with Katie, and answered Milly for her. 'Like, we could have all been sent home, had our horses taken away and never seen each other again.'

'Oh, yeah, there's always that,' said Milly with a laugh.

Katie continued to play around the mud's edge. She didn't even have her boots dirty yet.

'You going to help anytime soon?' asked Milly, who had obviously noticed Katie's clean clothes, too.

Katie squirmed on the spot, and Poppy laughed at her friend.

'I'll give you ten seconds,' said Poppy, grinning over at Milly.

'Ten seconds before what?' Katie whimpered back.

'Eight... nine... TEN,' giggled Poppy before flinging a bucket-load of grimy water all over Katie's 'Horse Mad' T-shirt.

'Argghhh!' Katie squealed and looked shocked as she stood there, dripping with muddy water.

Poppy bent double, she was laughing so hard. And Milly was in fits of laughter, too. Poppy's cheeks were aching, but she couldn't stop laughing. Within seconds, she was joining Milly in bombarding Katie with more water.

'I'll get you for that!' Katie screamed.

'Like how?' Milly was still roaring with laughter. 'We're already drenched.'

Poppy threw the bucket down and marched through the pools of water and mud. Katie looked at her sceptically but didn't move away.

'Come here,' ordered Poppy, putting her arm out to Katie to help her across the slippy mud.

Katie did as she was told, probably hoping to avoid another soaking, Poppy chuckled to herself, and Milly sprang over the gate to join them.

'We're in this together, right?' Poppy asked.

The other two nodded, both smiling.

'No more adventures, okay? Riding only,' she said to Milly.

'And no trying to get out of punishment jobs?' Milly added, her eyes trained on Katie.

'No more hare-brained ideas,' Katie snapped back.

Poppy placed one hand out in the middle, and watched as Milly's and then Katie's hands thumped on top.

'These next five days aren't going to be so bad,' Katie said. 'At least we're all still here, living the punishment together. We'll make it fun.'

'I guess,' agreed Milly.

'You guess?' said Katie.

'Yeah, it will be fun until we get to Sophie's practice gymkhana and the riding school kids beat us because we've had no practice,' Milly pointed out.

'But we're here and we'll all be in the same boat,' Katie said, echoing Poppy's thoughts. 'We didn't lose our ponies, so it's not the end of the world.'

'Yeah, Katie's right,' insisted Poppy. 'We've still got each other, I've still got Crystal and you two still have Cody and Joe.' She sighed. 'And Milly, the riding school kids are not crappy riders. They help to pay the bills around here.'

Poppy looked over to where Crystal and the other two ponies were grazing in the next paddock. You know, Aunt Sophie never said anything about not being able to ride our ponies bareback,' suggested Poppy with a mischievous grin on her face. She didn't want to get into trouble again, *no way*, but she was itching to ride, and her aunt and uncle were both up at the stables, so they'd never know.

Milly's face lit up at that, but Katie wasn't convinced.

'No, no, no!' Katie insisted. 'No more trouble, I thought we'd just agreed.'

'Come on, no one will ever know,' Milly said.

'Yeah, I've heard that before.'

Poppy jumped up, jods plastered to her legs, hair wet from the water fight. 'Come on, race you to the gate!'

Milly sprinted fast ahead of her, and Katie – although reluctantly – ran, too.

'Last one on a pony has to finish off the water troughs!' yelled Poppy.

CHAPTER SEVENTEEN

Back in the Saddle

'That was the longest five days ever,' Milly declared.

Poppy had to agree. It had been tough not being allowed to ride their ponies, but they were making up for it now. She nudged Crystal in the side, urging her to go faster. She burst into a canter, and Poppy slipped one hand off the reins and down to pat her neck, biting her bottom lip to stop from laughing as they shot past a shocked Milly and Joe. Milly's shout only spurred her on, and Crystal cleared the fallen log in the track before Milly and Joe had a chance to catch them.

Katie called out from behind. 'Wait up!'

Poppy slowed Crystal down and giggled as Milly

poked her tongue out at her. She looked at Joe, knowing how he liked to ride upfront at all times, and thought he seemed equally unimpressed about not jumping first.

'It seems like forever ago that we jumped that log for the first time,' Poppy said.

Katie had caught up now and stopped beside them as Poppy halted Crystal. 'Or that we rode over there.' Katie pointed, and Poppy's gaze followed her finger. She gulped as she stared over the tops of the bushes and toward the old gate they'd jumped to get onto Old Smithy's land.

'I still can't believe we actually found those horses,' Poppy said.

'Or that we didn't get sent home,' Milly added.

Poppy leaned forward and slung her arms around Crystal's neck, stroking her soft hair. 'I'm gonna miss you guys, even if it is only for a few days.' She was looking forward to getting home, to seeing her mum and giving her brother a big hug. But she was going to miss Crystal and her friends big time.

'Me too,' Katie said.

Milly just smiled, and Poppy smiled back.

'Are your parents coming to the practice gymkhana tomorrow?' Katie asked Milly.

'Yeah. Although I don't think they'll come 'til later in the afternoon, and then I'll just go home with them,' Milly said.

Poppy stroked Crystal's mane absently, feeling sad that her mum and dad wouldn't be there to watch her in the gymkhana. But she was happy for her friends, that their parents were coming, and forced herself to smile.

'Aunt Sophie's taking me home on Monday morning,' she added.

They were all silent. Poppy wondered if the other two were thinking about how much they'd miss their ponies.

'Ready to ride back?' Katie asked.

Poppy nodded and sat up straight in the saddle again, realising that both Katie and Milly were looking at her. 'Yeah, let's go,' she said, groaning when a smile spread across Milly's face. She knew that grin, and it always came before trouble.

'Last one back's a rotten rat!' Milly yelled, kicking Joe in the side and cantering over toward the log.

Poppy exchanged glances with Katie, and they both burst out laughing and raced after Milly, side by side. Still wearing a smile, Poppy felt better than she had in ages. She thought back on all that had happened the past week, and knew that telling her aunt about what was going on with her mum had been the right thing to do. She trusted her to help.

As she rode alongside Katie, she realised how relieved she was that her friends now knew what had happened to her dad. It was like a huge weight had been lifted, and she was free to be a kid again. They might have almost got sent home, thought Poppy, but it was still the best holiday she'd ever had.

ABOUT THE AUTHOR

As a horse-crazy girl, Soraya dreamed of owning her own pony and riding every day. For years, pony books like *The Saddle Club* had to suffice, until she finally convinced her parents to buy her a horse. There were plenty of adventures on horseback throughout her childhood, and lots of stories scribbled in notebooks, which eventually became inspiration for Soraya's very own pony series. Soraya now lives with her husband and children on a small farm in her native New Zealand, surrounded by four-legged friends and still vividly recalling what it felt like to be 12 years old and head over heels in love with horses.

'Hands high' (hh) is the measurement usually used to measure horses, with 14.2 hh being the largest pony – anything taller is classified as a horse. Horse owners used to measure with their own hands, from thumb to little finger, to estimate a horse's size, but that wasn't very accurate as different owners had different-sized hands. And so, today, one hand is considered to be exactly 4 inches. To get the most accurate measurement, horses are measured with a measuring stick when standing on concrete, from the ground to their withers (shoulder blades).

Different horse breeds are bred for different purposes, based on their qualities. The Welsh breed is known for producing easy-going, showy, talented ponies, while the Arabians are sensitive, energetic horses with beautiful paces. To get the best of both breeds, some horses are crossbred. Like Crystal, crossbred horses are suitable for a wide range of disciplines, including showing, jumping and dressage, as well as general riding.

ACKNOWLEDGEMENTS

Penguin Random House would like to give special thanks to Isabella Carter, Emily Mitchell and India James Timms – the faces of Poppy, Milly and Katie on the book covers.

Special thanks must also go to Trish, Caroline, Ben and the team at Valley Park Riding School, Templestowe, Victoria, for their tremendous help in hosting the photoshoot for the covers at Valley Park, and, of course, to the four-legged stars: Alfie and Joe from Valley Park Riding School, and Carinda Park Vegas and his owner Annette Vellios.

Thank you, too, to Caitlin Maloney from Ragamuffin Pet Photography for taking the perfect shots that are the covers.